TORN

BOOK THREE IN THE DEVIL'S DEVIANTS SERIES.

Gladys Cross

TORN, THE DEVILS DEVIANTS MC
ASIN: B0CLL1CQSR   ISBN: 9798878083676

Cover design by: Rocking Book Covers
Editing by: Revision Division, Kimberly Hunt

THE DEVIANTS
San Antonio Charter

Pops, Founder
Ryder, President
Hunter, Vice President
Tweak, Secretary
Gunner, Treasurer
Beast, Road Captain
Mad Dog, Original Member
Dagger, Original Member
Colt, Member
Marco, Prospect
Switch, Nomad
Cannon, Deceased

STELLA

Our story was like an old book, dog-eared and worn from all the ways we'd tried to hurt each other over the years. Switch was determined to restore each page while I wanted to watch it burn. There was no way we could tape back together all the pages that had been **Torn**.

AUTHOR'S NOTE:

Torn is a dark MC romance and may contain subject matter that might offend sensitive readers. In this series you can expect to encounter violence, murder, death, profanity, rape, explicit sexual situations with BDSM themes, drugs, tobacco use, PTSD, references to mental health, suspense, crime, and characters with questionable morals. Reader discretion is advised.

* Torn is the third book in the series and contains spoilers for the previous books.*
The Devil's Deviants MC
#1 Defiant
#2 Damaged

Don't forget to sign up to my newsletter for upcoming releases.

CHAPTER 1

SWITCH

A drum beat a steady rhythm at the back of my skull and my mouth felt like someone had shoved half a dozen cotton balls into it. When I blinked, a shaft of light pierced my eyes, and I sat up, the blanket pooling around my waist. The room tilted sideways on its axis, and I rubbed the heel of my hand into my eye, hoping that would help.

When the world finally righted itself, I almost wished it hadn't.

From beside me, the blanket shifted, and I caught a faint whiff of strawberries, making me want to hurl. Not that I had anything against berries, exactly, but it wasn't vanilla mixed with motor oil and paint. My favorite scent in the entire world. The one I missed more than anything.

But the smell, like the woman it belonged to, would remain a ghost from my past. A ghost that continued to haunt me even after all these long months apart.

My pack of cigarettes beckoned to me from the nightstand, but my cell phone vibrated from beside them. I looked down at the display. Speaking of past ghosts.

"It's been a long time, Ryder," I said, keeping my voice low.

The lump beside me moaned, the sound distinctly feminine, but it wasn't the sexy rasp that always made blood rush to my cock.

I swung my legs over the side of the bed and stood, pleased that the contents of my stomach stayed put. Clothes littered the floor, and I tripped on my way to the bathroom, stubbing my toe on the end of the bed.

Silently I cursed so I wouldn't wake up Mindy, or was it Mallory, fuck, I didn't even know. It didn't matter, anyway. She'd curse me for not being able to remember it and storm out in a huff. Women were always thinking they could fix you like you were some broken doll. But none of them could fix what ailed me.

Hobbling into the bathroom, I quietly shut

the door behind me.

"Jesus, Switch, are you drunk? It's barely ten o'clock in the morning, for fuck's sake."

Sobriety had become a dirty word for me, one that only surfaced long enough for me to attend club business. The rest of the time I didn't want to remember. It was bad enough she haunted my dreams. I didn't need her fucking with my head while I was awake.

But Ryder would never understand that. How could he? His girl hadn't told him to fuck off after he'd gone and messed it all up in a fit of ignorance.

"I'm still hungover, asshole, but thanks for asking." Which was sorta true. I passed out, or was it blacked out, not sure which, sometime after four. So, technically, I wasn't drunk. "Was there something you needed, or did you call just to bust my balls?"

He sighed. "Yeah, I need you to get your ass sobered up and be prepared to set all the bullshit aside."

Ryder wanted to magically squash the beef he had with me? Yeah, I wasn't buying it. Something was up. When I left, I did it knowing he'd probably never forgive me. The man held on to a grudge like a baby with a bottle.

"What the fuck are you talking about?"

"I hate like hell that the first time we're speaking to each other in months is under such shitty circumstances. But I had to call. For

8

Stella."

His voice caught on her name, betraying his emotions, and my chest tightened painfully. The meager contents of my stomach threatened to make a comeback. Now I knew something was seriously wrong. Fuck. Not my girl. Anything but her.

"Switch, Stella's been missing for over a week."

His words drove me to my knees, the cold tile against my bare flesh forcing me not to black out, to stay in the moment. Even if what he was about to say tore me to shreds. Well, even more than what he'd already said. I needed to focus on his words.

"Hunter wants to wait until nightfall and slip in undetected. If we go in guns blazing, and he's wrong, then we risk them either moving her or cutting their losses. Since I'm not willing to chance it, the club will hang back and watch the perimeter until Hunter gives us the go ahead."

My grip on the chipped countertop tightened, the whites of my knuckles a stark contrast against the dark surface. Someone had taken my Stel, my reason for breathing, and they were gonna pay. We would get her back. We had to. Failure wasn't an option if my world was to keep on spinning.

"Which of our enemies has her?"

I could still hear him breathing into the phone, so I knew he hadn't hung up, but he wasn't saying anything either. Shit. Stella wasn't some sweet butt or club whore. She was the daughter of a founding member. Not that we'd ever condone someone fucking with any of the girls under our protection.

That told me whoever had her either had giant cojones or had no clue who in the hell we were. Either way, my best friend owed me some answers and my patience with his bullshit was at an end.

"Tell me!"

As my voice echoed back to me in the tiny space, I knew there was no way in hell I was letting Hunter go in alone. The blood of our enemies would drip from my fingertips by the time this day was out. All they had to do was point me in the right direction.

"Switch, it wasn't our enemies that took her. It was a human trafficking ring."

CHAPTER 2

STELLA

A MONTH EARLIER…

"Fuck no."

The words hung heavy between us as I stared out the window, watching the pool shimmer in the early morning light. The hedges that surrounded it were all trimmed in perfectly straight, symmetrical lines. A tree limb overhead swayed in the breeze, but there was probably a gardener out there somewhere whose job it was to make sure no leaves fell onto the water's still surface.

This place was more of a museum than a home. Signed paintings adorned the walls, and he had artwork displayed in glass cases or sitting atop marble columns. More than once I'd thought about turning a statue on its side just to see how long it took his staff to fix it.

I would applaud their level of efficiency if it didn't utterly creep me out. Who ironed paint-stained coveralls or neatly folded a thong? Not that I'd ever asked for them to do any of it. My clothes would be on the floor when I went to sleep and in the morning they'd be in the chair by the door.

"What do you mean fuck no," he bit out, his Spanish accent thickening around the word no as if he wanted to strangle it.

Hell, he probably did. Men didn't like to hear the word no, and Antonio Sanchez was a man used to having people obey his every command, often while they kissed his ass. It was really rather nauseating, and it took a massive amount of effort for me to refrain from making gagging noises.

Other girls might go gaga over being with a man that had that kind of wealth and power, but it didn't mean shit to me. We had an understanding. He distracted me whenever I needed it, and in return I didn't make any demands or ask any questions.

Most of the time, our arrangement worked. Then again, he'd never tried to keep me here.

Crossing my arms, I turned to face him. "Just because I called you papi once in the sack doesn't mean you can tell me what to do."

His lips twitched despite the cold fury lurking in the depths of his dark eyes. "I'll try to keep that in mind. Unfortunately, it doesn't change the fact that my enemies have figured out who you are and what you mean to me. Until I can track down the source of the leak, I need you to remain here for your own protection."

I snorted. "You know who my father is. Do you really think this is the first time I've ever been in danger?"

"The authorities constantly breathing down your father's neck is hardly the same thing," he pointed out as he smoothed his hand down a navy suit jacket that probably cost more than my rent.

The nerve of this motherfucker. That's okay, he'd soon learn that he couldn't boss me around like the trust fund babies and socialites that had graced his bed before me. My tiara was made from twisted metal and thorns, not gold and diamonds. I was the daughter of a biker, born with the wind in my face, and I didn't do hemmed in. No matter the danger.

Antonio's enemies, whoever they were, couldn't be any worse than my father's. His club, even back when he was VP, distributed more drugs than all the various mafia families combined. So, it was never just about the authorities. When you were at the top of the food chain, there were a lot of hungry wolves constantly nipping at your heels.

"You're right." I sauntered up to him, a sickeningly sweet smile plastered on my face.

If he'd known anything at all about me, aside from how to give me the occasional orgasm, he'd know this didn't spell good things for him.

"The DEA is my only concern nowadays, but there was a time when that wasn't the case. Back when my father was VP, I had to worry about some asshole using me to tear down the club he helped build."

His dark brow furrowed as I gazed up at him, my hand smoothing out the breast of his suit jacket. "Do you know what my father gave me for my sweet sixteen?"

"A motorcycle?"

"Good guess, but no."

Pain sliced through my chest as images of Switch and me, side by side, bent over the bike my father dragged home from the junkyard assailed me. We worked for hours on end trying to get that piece of shit to start because my father had said if I could get it running, I could ride it. Thirteen-year-old me had wanted that first taste of freedom almost as much as I'd wanted Switch to kiss me.

After a couple of deep breaths, I shoved those memories back into the dark recesses of my mind, hoping they would never again see the light of day. They belonged hidden among the graveyard of useless facts I carried around with me, like most car horns are in the key of F, because it didn't matter. At least, not anymore.

"He gave me a *Beretta Pico 380* with the club's emblem on the grip." His eyes followed the motion of my hand as I patted the pocket of my overalls, his brow arched at the visible outline of the butt of the gun. "He taught me to shoot it too. Would you like a demonstration before I head over to the shop?"

"Since you obviously can't be reasoned with," he growled low in his throat. "Jules will have to watch over you."

"I don't need a babysitter." To emphasize my point, I patted my pocket again, the gun's weight against my side reassuring.

"Jules will watch over you, with or without your consent." He bit out each word, his fists clenched at his sides. "I have enough going on right now without having to deal with blowback from your father's club because you refused to listen and wound up dead."

A vein stuck out in stark contrast against the tan skin of his corded neck, and I had the strangest desire to poke the beast.

"Fine, but he'll have to do it from the bitch seat of my bike. If the guys ask, I'll just tell 'em my new man prefers to be ridden."

His nostrils flared for a brief second before the corner of his lip curled upward. It wasn't exactly a sneer, but it didn't hold enough warmth to be considered a smile, either.

"Tell them whatever you like as long as you arrive there in the back of my armored Maybach."

Yeah, right. Like I was going to let the guys catch me pulling up to the garage all *Driving Miss Daisy* style in a two hundred-thousand-dollar car.

"I'd rather take the bullet, thanks. Your man can follow me around if that helps you sleep at night, but I draw the line at being chauffeured." Brushing past him, I yanked open the massive oak door, and hollered over my shoulder, "If he's not on my bike in five, I'm leaving without him."

My boots squeaked against the freshly polished dark hardwood floors as I moved down the hall, but it wasn't until I stood at the top of the main staircase that I heard the echo of dress shoes behind me. He could follow me all he liked, but I wasn't about to change my mind. Not about this. My mother spent most of her life letting a man dictate where she went. And for what? In the end, it was cancer that took her, not a bullet.

Frederick wore his usual bland expression as he swung open one side of the wooden doors when I reached the bottom. Yes, in this day and age, Antonio had an honest to goodness butler complete with tails, gloves, and bowtie. It didn't matter if I came over at midnight or four in the afternoon; he was always the one who opened the door for me. Sometimes I wondered if the old man ever left his post.

"Have a good day, miss," he said, his tone dry, the end of his nose pointed downward.

Antonio's dress shoes scraped against the pavement as he continued to follow me down the long driveway. My gun was heavy in my pocket, and while shooting him in the foot was tempting, it would be a shame to risk messing up the new candy apple red paint job on his *Maserati*. It was some of my best work. You couldn't even tell someone had run into the back of it.

I spun on my heel, prepared to give him hell, only to come face to face with Lurch from *The Adam's Family*. What the fuck?

"Uh, can I help you?"

He folded his arms in front of him, his pale hands overlapping at his waist. "I'm your new bodyguard, Jules."

Shit. This was the guy Antonio sent to watch over me? Laughter bubbled up my throat and spilled out of me as I tried to picture his elongated frame on the back of my bike.

"I thought Antonio told you."

He sounded like a kid who'd taken a hit off the helium tank at a birthday party, and it only made me laugh harder.

"You're in real danger, you know," he huffed as I bent over, holding my side.

"Sorry...I was just picturing"—I sucked in a

breath—"you on the back...of my bike."

I peered up at him in time to see his nod of understanding, a smile transforming the harsh angles of his face.

"Even if I could fit, it's not a smart idea for you to be riding around on a bike."

My laughter died a sudden death. If Antonio thought he'd send this behemoth of a man out here to intimidate me into doing what he wanted, he was dead wrong. The club had Beast, who was a giant man, same as Jules, so his size didn't faze me.

Not that I was one to knuckle under when faced with male aggression. I'd grown up dealing with that shit.

"Listen, Jules. Let's get one thing straight. I don't need or want a babysitter. I only agreed to let you tag along—"

He tackled me to the ground, my words cutting off as we landed hard, my breath coming out in a whoosh. My head somehow ended up cradled in one of Jules's massive mitts, but the rest of my body hurt something fierce.

Jules rolled us onto the driveway a second before I heard the unmistakable rat-a-tat-tat of a machine gun. Chunks from the patch of grass we'd been lying on moments ago flew into the air.

"Roll under the car!" he shouted into my ear amid another flurry of rat-a-tat-tats.

My brain misfired, and I lay there on the

pavement, frozen.

"Move your ass," Jules huffed as he began shoving me underneath the car.

His rough hands on my body were enough to break through the fog of fear that had held me in its thrall. Rocking my body back and forth, I shimmied the rest of the way under, leaving just enough room for his larger frame to follow behind. A scream threatened to tear up my throat, but I swallowed it down, afraid I'd give away our hiding spot.

Jules curled himself around me in our confined space, the sounds of gunfire all around us. With the constant barrage of noise, I couldn't even pinpoint which direction it was coming from anymore making it unlikely we'd remain in one piece for very long.

God had always remained an abstract concept for me. Neither of my parents were the religious sort, so I wasn't sure what made me think of him now. Maybe it was because I was coming face to face with death for the first time. If that were the case, I had only one regret, and it had nothing to do with not taking advantage of Antonio's gilded prison.

The gunfire ceased, the absence of noise after the chaos of moments ago almost deafening. We lay there, huddled together, still, waiting. For what, I wasn't sure, but I wasn't about to move until Jules told me to. He could have easily left me to die on the front lawn, job or not, yet he hadn't.

Dark eyes met mine, a ghost of a smile on his lips. This fucker was clearly mental, and I'd put my faith in him. Blindly, I might add. It made me think of my best friend, Brandy. Maybe she had it right after all. She'd fallen for the craziest, most dangerous man I knew, and she was blissfully happy.

"Care to go inside now?"

His words were a slap in the face. Jules would definitely not be the knight in shining armor who carried me off into the sunset. Moment of insanity gone. But the man had kept me alive, and I wasn't about to spit in his face by being reckless.

"No, but I will let you give me a ride to the clubhouse."

CHAPTER 3

STELLA

"So, you and Lurch, huh?" Tweak's dark head popped up over the trunk of a *Chevy Impala*, the bent plastic bumper he'd torn off still in his hand. Plastic skidded across the cement as he tossed it aside and asked, "Should we expect this douche train you've been riding to get off the tracks soon? Asking for a friend."

"A friend or friends?" He shook his head, his signature dimple giving him away. "Yeah, that's what I thought. The club is worse than a bunch of sorority sisters at a slumber party."

He threw his head back and laughed, the

sound competing with the heavy metal coming from the speaker beside me. Asshole. The lot of them were, but they were my assholes and I'd do anything to protect them. Which was why I couldn't let on that Jules and I were hardly an item. He was more like a tampon—functional and necessary, yet you wished he wasn't there.

"Come on. You can't be serious about this guy. He dresses like a funeral home director and watches you like he's afraid someone is going to steal you."

Tweak, and his cousin, Ryder, with their tousled hair and chiseled physiques, were like catnip for women. Ryder's sense of responsibility to the club his father helped build lent him more of a brooding I-don't-give-a-fuck quality, while Tweak openly flaunted his magazine worthy looks. He presented himself to the world as a charming playboy, but I'd always seen beyond his charisma to the understated shrewdness that lies beneath.

All the guys had been worried about me after Switch left the club, but he'd been the only one to see that I needed an outlet for all the rage I had stored up. He'd taken the screaming, wrench throwing, and even the hexing of his manhood in stride. For me.

But this he couldn't help me with. I'd gotten myself involved with a man I shouldn't have, and now I had to put on my big girl panties and deal with the mess I'd made of my life.

So, I raised an eyebrow and pasted on what I hoped was a smirk. I'd never consciously tried to recreate something that came as naturally to me as breathing. It felt strange on my face, but I ignored the sinking feeling in my gut to concentrate on punctuating my expression with words.

"You can tell all the asshats upstairs that I'm quite serious about what he can do with that monster cock of his, so you guys better get used to seeing his ugly mug around here."

The look on his face was honestly priceless. If I had to describe it, I'd say it was a cross between a gag and a cough with a dash of curiosity mixed in. The guys hadn't been lying. Tweak really was a big ol' freak. Which was saying something, considering the shit I'd witnessed at the clubhouse over the years.

Come to think of it, maybe that was why my tastes leaned toward dangerous men who were more likely to bend me over a chair than whisper sweet nothings in my ear. Vanilla was boring, but in my case, it would have also kept me out of trouble. Instead, I was stuck lying to my family and friends about my creepy shadow.

Damn. Speak of the devil. The towering frame of my jailer filled the doorway, and I looked down at my watch. Six o'clock, on the dot. He didn't trust me not to outmaneuver him, not that I blamed him. I'd fought his presence in my life like a hellcat and lost. Miserably.

That didn't mean I was going to take my defeat lying down. No, I would take every opportunity I could to make him suffer for following Antonio's orders. Maybe that made me a bitch, considering he'd saved my life, but I needed an outlet for the resentment that simmered in my blood like lava.

We'd been joined at the hip for three weeks now, and during that time I'd learned a thing or two about Jules. He drank *Red Bull* the way some people drank water, he always smelled of fine Cuban cigars even though I'd never actually seen him smoke one, and he didn't like to be touched. Ever. Anywhere, anytime, for any reason.

Setting down the wrench in my hand, I sauntered up to him, enjoying the way his lips thinned as he watched my approach. When I stopped directly in front of him, he tensed, but didn't take a step back. Mainly because we both knew he couldn't.

This bit of payback was the only control I had over the situation I'd found myself in, and damn if I wouldn't wield that motherfucker like a sword. His swift intake of breath as my blunt fingertips trailed up the lapel of his suit jacket was a satisfying jab, but I wasn't done twisting the blade. I needed him to suffer as I did. To feel trapped the way I did.

With his towering height, the only way I was going to reach him was on my tiptoes. Fine with me. I'd become a goddamn ballerina if I had to.

He leaned back as I drew closer, forcing me to either concede to a peck on the cheek, which I wasn't about to do, or contort my body to reach him. We might have needed to keep up appearances for the sake of the club, but he wasn't about to make it easy for me to capitalize on his weakness.

His breath fanned over the bridge of my nose, the smoky and sweet aroma of tobacco, leather, wood, and spices filling my lungs. Our lips had barely brushed when I felt a shudder work itself through his body.

He couldn't help his reaction any more than I'd been able to stop the tears that were streaming down my face when he barged in on me in the bathroom this morning. We still wouldn't be even, but this minor victory would have to tide me over. For now.

Jules's left eye twitched as he watched the heels of my boots kiss the cement and I wondered if he was even aware of the small tell. My guess would be no, and I filed that away along with everything else I knew about him because sometimes it was the minor details that tripped people up. Anything I could use to escape his watchful eye, I would.

"Are you ready to go?"

His question was more for Tweak's benefit than mine. We both knew I didn't have a choice in the matter. As they say, the show must go on.

"Ready as I'll ever be."

CHAPTER 4

STELLA

The gentle thud of the bass vibrated through the speakers surrounding our booth, its familiarity soothing. We were tucked away in the roped off area of the second floor VIP section. The music here was low enough that you didn't have to lean in to be heard, yet loud enough that the servers couldn't easily eavesdrop.

Pretty young things sashed by now and then, flirting as they refilled drink orders. Well-dressed men who thought way too much of themselves puffed on cigars as they bragged to one another about their toys.

My jailer kept a close eye on me from the opposite corner, his arms crossed in front of him, his usual frown permanently etched into his face.

And me? When I looked down, I didn't even recognize myself. Thin gold chains held up either side of my severely plunging neckline. You couldn't wear a bra with this dress because the cut out in the back ended at the top of my ass. The slit revealed way more of my thigh than any man I wasn't fucking had any right to see, and my feet were pinched into gold strappy sandals that matched my dress. In short, I was in hell.

Antonio had insisted that his bait be wrapped in a tempting package. Easy for him to say, he wasn't the one with tape on his chest holding his tits in place. Nothing about this plan of his made me feel comfortable, but he was right about one thing. We were out of options.

He still hadn't found the source of the leak in his security, and nobody had tried for me since the shooting. His enemies had gone radio silent, not that either of us was fooled into thinking they'd forgotten about me. They were merely waiting for the perfect opportunity to strike. Tonight, we would give it to them.

Antonio had hired additional security from an outside agency for the night and planted them all throughout the club. Not even Jules knew who they were or where they'd be. Antonio said Jules was here for appearance's sake, but he hadn't fooled me for a second. Jules was his backup plan, and while I had fought him on most things, this would not have been one of them. The man might be perpetually on my shit list, but it made me feel better to have him here, watching my back.

Antonio might have been a dangerous man, one easily capable of killing, but I wasn't stupid enough to trust him. I knew what our relationship was, and what it wasn't. He'd kept Jules with me for his own peace of mind more than my safety. I'd seen and heard enough to know he wasn't as he appeared, and he didn't know yet if he could trust me to keep my mouth shut.

No, if shit hit the fan tonight, and I suspected it would, I needed someone who was willing and capable of keeping me alive. It galled me to rely on Jules when I could protect myself, but there was no help for it. The scrap of fabric I wore wouldn't conceal a thigh holster, and a knife wasn't much use in a gunfight.

The man to my right casually placed his hand on my thigh and leaned in closer. His breath caressed my ear, and a shiver worked its way down my body. This fucker had about a second before I twisted his wrist to a very unpleasant angle. I might even laugh while I listened to the bone snap.

Antonio must have caught on to what I was thinking, because his dark eyes narrowed before he subtly shook his head. He didn't have to remind me. I was bait. Window dressing. If I broke a man's arm, then I would draw unwanted attention to myself, defeating the entire purpose of tonight. All that planning, effort, and time wasted. I had to act natural when this entire situation was anything but.

"I never understood what Antonio saw in you until tonight. Seeing you in that dress makes me wish I had overlooked your dreadful attire and snapped you up first."

This was his best pickup line. Really? He was a douchey prick that was a little too picky given his paunch and wrinkles. With lines like that, he must have to pay through the nose to get women into bed. A minor consolation given his hand was trying to inch up my thigh.

"I guess I got lucky."

If my frosty tone fazed him, he didn't let on, choosing to remain all up in my personal space. What I wouldn't give to tell this tiny-dicked, obnoxious little weasel that he could go fuck himself because nobody else wanted to. After I punched him in the nuts.

"For now," he said with a leer before removing the hand that rested on my thigh.

A shiver of revulsion slid down my spine at his implied threat. Fuck him and fuck Antonio. They could measure their dicks while I sidled up to the bar. I'd still be out in the open for all to see, but I wouldn't have to deal with this shit.

"If you'll excuse me, I'm going to powder my nose and refresh my drink."

The lecherous douche slid his eyes down my body once more before getting up so I could slide out of the booth. Hope he enjoyed the view from the back because that was all he would get to see of me for the rest of the night. My stupid heels gave him quite a view as I stood, and it wasn't like I could walk normally. Soak it all in, asshole.

"Fucking heels," I muttered under my breath as I strolled away from the table.

Wouldn't it be something if I went ass over teacup and ended up giving him a free show? Heels and I didn't get along. The things were unnatural torture devices thought up by men. Them and pantyhose. Maybe we ought to invent something uncomfortable for them to wear in public.

As I teetered down the long hallway that led to the bathrooms in my high heels, all manner of devious things crossed my mind. My favorite was crocheted short shorts that constantly made their junk itch.

With a snort, I pushed open the bathroom door and headed over to the row of sinks. Even here it was dimly lit, shadows playing off the dark paneling.

The porcelain sinks were like the lights on a lighthouse, breaking up the gloom, pulling you in. I leaned against one, letting out a strained breath as I stared into the mirror.

How the hell had I let this happen? No distraction was worth getting killed over. Or was it?

My dreams never let me rest. He was always there, haunting in his beauty. How I still craved the sight of him. Pathetic really, to be pining after a man who didn't want you. He just didn't want anyone else to have me, either. He'd even hid it well, using my father as an excuse.

The words "Switch loves Stella" scrawled across the wall in the garage had been what did me in. Gutted me. And there was no taking back what I said to him that day. It was the reason he left and never came back. Fuck off. Such a simple phrase to cause so much destruction.

Water splashed against my face as I tried to erase the look on his face from my mind. Like I'd ever be able to forget how his lips thinned and the depths of his cinnamon eyes swam with pain. It was his eyes. They got me every time.

Blotting my face with a paper towel, I resolved to get my shit together. To leave the past where it belonged, in the past. One day the memories wouldn't be so sharp, cutting me to the quick. One day I'd forget.

At least that was the lie I'd tell myself so I could put one high-heeled foot in front of the other. Time to take this shit show to the bar.

The door swung out, and I walked into a solid wall of muscle. At first, I thought it was Jules coming to check on me, but the shadows playing across his face were all wrong. Lights sunk into the ceiling above us made him look like he had a halo suspended above his springy gold hair.

A glint of metal caught my eye right before I felt the prick against the side of my neck. Son of a bitch. My limbs were already growing heavy as he eased me closer to his chest, my eyes searching for help over his shoulder. Jules stood not two feet away, but I could tell something was wrong even before I saw the blade cutting into his neck.

The four of us were the only ones in the hallway. Aside from the throbbing pulse of the base, it was oddly quiet. Where was the security Antonio hired for the night? If I was their primary aim, why weren't they storming down the hall to kill these two assholes who had gotten the drop on Jules?

My vision was growing fuzzy around the edges as the realization that Jules and I were in trouble sank in. I wanted to fight, to claw, to tear their eyes out, to do something, anything to save us. My body, however, refused to do anything I wanted it to do. Inside my head, I raged and screamed even as the blackness licked at my mind, threatening to pull me under.

As the man dragged me past Jules, my head lolled to the side, my eyes locking on him. Jules was always so stoic, except for the times I'd fucked with him by touching him. Now, though, remorse was etched into every plane of his angular face.

"I'm sorry, Stella," he whispered in his annoyingly high-pitched voice. "I had no other choice."

The last of his words followed me into the sinking abyss of darkness. Then there was nothing.

CHAPTER 5

SWITCH

Cherry's face brightened when she saw me walk through the door, the rag she'd been using to wipe down the bar frozen in midair. With the way I ran out on the club, she was likely to be the only friendly face I'd find here. Not that I'd let a frosty welcome deter me any.

Stel was all that mattered right now, and for her, I'd take whatever shit they wanted to shovel at my feet. Anything to have her back where she belonged, safely among her family, tinkering in the shop she loved.

Pain hit me square in the chest as I

envisioned all the shit she might have had to endure since being taken, and I staggered the last few steps to the bar, grateful there was something to keep me upright.

Cherry's smile fell, and she set her rag down, cautiously moving closer. She was smart. She recognized a wounded animal when she saw one. Tentatively she lifted her tiny hand, setting it down on my thickly veined one.

"Hunter will get our girl back." Her hazel eyes were glassy as she shook her head up and down, her blond curls bouncing with the force of her conviction. "He would never break a promise he made to Brandy."

Who the fuck was this Brandy chick? Never mind. It wasn't important. Hunter's promises didn't mean shit to me because I would be the one going after my girl, not him. All I had to do was keep my cool around the club long enough to get the intel I needed, then I'd be on my way.

A door swung open, the muted chatter of men floating into the room. Cherry looked over my shoulder, nodded once, and met my eyes again. She gave my hand a squeeze, the pressure surprisingly strong for a girl who couldn't weigh more than a buck twenty soaking wet.

"We'll catch up later. The sooner you meet with the boys, the sooner you can give Stella a hug for me. She won't like it"—Cherry gave me a watery smile—"but tell her it's that or I cart her off to the nail salon when she gets back."

My knuckles stood out against the metal of the bar as I gripped its edge, trying to rein in the riot of emotions that threatened to swallow me whole. Cherry was the sweetest person I'd ever met, and I wasn't so far gone that I didn't recognize that she was only trying to help. But I couldn't dwell on what I'd lost and keep a clear head.

Yet, I couldn't seem to help myself. A memory of Stella standing in the shop, holding her nails up to the light, fine lines forming between her dark blond brows flashed behind my eyelids. Her full pink lips would part just before she let fly a string of curse words that would make a sailor blush.

When she was done with her tirade, I'd always tell her the same thing, that I liked her nails best when they had grease or paint staining the tips. She'd shoot me a snarky sideways glance, then turn her head to hide the ghost of a smile touching her lips. Knowing I was the one to put it there made me hard every damn time.

But memories wouldn't bring her back, so I forced myself to set aside the pain and focus on the present. Cherry had always been there for me when the desire I kept locked inside became too much to bear alone, and she never asked for anything in return. She didn't deserve for me to be a dick, even though a part of me wanted to lash out at her. Anything to shift the blame away from where it belonged, squarely on my shoulders.

"I'll pass along the message," I said with a fake-ass smile, my voice gravelly from a combination of disuse and alcohol.

Shit. If I was going to get Stel back, I needed to get a handle on all the fucked-up shit that was swirling around inside my head. The broken fucker that had walked through those doors wouldn't do her a damn bit of good, and I had a lot to make up for. Starting with not being there when she'd needed me the most.

I turned to face the doorway, already knowing Ryder would be standing there. My best friend. My only friend, really, until he'd introduced me to Stella.

There was a reason I kept my circle small when I was younger. Hiding bruises wasn't as hard when there was no one that gave a shit about you. Stel had blown that out of the water the day she'd stopped by our trailer and caught my old man laying into me out front.

She'd taken one look at my battered face and let her most prized possession, the motorcycle I'd helped her rebuild a few years earlier, fall to the pavement. The battle cry she let out hadn't even finished echoing off the piece of shit truck parked across our lawn when she launched herself at him, her tiny fists pounding his back.

She was beautiful in her rage, and I knew at that moment that I'd do anything for her. Even fuck off if she ever asked me to.

Ryder never asked why Mad Dog took me in, and since Pops said the fewer people who knew about what happened the better, I wasn't about to enlighten him. The club had always protected its own and somewhere along the way, I'd forgotten that rule. She'd saved me, turned my life around, and I wasn't there when she was in trouble.

Never again. Whether she liked it or not, I was never leaving her side. Anyone who dared to say shit to me about it could fuck right the hell off. I didn't expect them to let me back into the club, I knew I'd burned that bridge, but if they were smart, they'd stay the fuck out of my way. Stel was mine, and it was about damn time I lay claim to her.

Ryder must have sensed the direction my thoughts had taken because he raised a dark brow. His shoulders blocked the doorway, separating me from the club.

He looked me up and down, but I wasn't sure what he hoped to find. If he was looking for an apology, he'd be waiting a long damn time. My regrets had nothing to do with the club. I'd choose her over them every time, without question.

"You look about as good as a pickled cat turd."

He'd always had an interesting way of wording shit. I wasn't exactly sure what a pickled cat turd looked like, nor did I want to, but I couldn't hate on him for the description. It probably fit right about now.

My beard was untrimmed, my T-shirt was wrinkled to hell and back, my usually slicked-back hair hung limply in my face, and I was pretty sure the bags under my eyes had bags. About the only thing on me that looked cared for was my cut.

Ryder's dark eyes narrowed on the patch below my name. Nomad. Not the Tucson charter. When I'd gone to my president, he'd given me a choice. I could either ride out on the next drug run or go nomad.

He never thought I'd rip off my patch and walk out. The life of a nomad was dangerous. No men at your side, but all the same enemies. What he didn't understand was that nothing could keep me from coming to get her. For her, I would gladly burn the world down.

Ryder's eyes wandered back up to meet mine, and I could see the pain clearly reflected in them. I wished I could say I wouldn't hurt him again, but I knew that was a lie. I'd be forced at some point to twist the knife I'd already sunk into his back, and for that, I was truly sorry. But it didn't sit right with me to rely on another man to save what I should have protected.

"Good. Lets me know I made the right decision in calling you."

He turned around, giving me his back, and pain filled my chest knowing that he might later regret those words. Most people thought I left and never looked back, but the reality was far uglier. I was a shadow of the man I once was, and all because I'd never truly left. My heart had remained in San Antonio, tearing my spirit in two.

When I entered, the room descended into silence. Every man turned toward me, the heat of their glares palpable. Well, everyone but the new prospect who viewed me with curiosity rather than open hostility.

That was okay, though. They could tell me to fuck off with their eyes, I admitted to deserving their ire. I'd left them in their darkest hour for Stella, and if she asked me to, I'd drop them all again in a heartbeat. There was no room in my heart for remorse because it was near to bursting for Stel. Always for Stel.

Beast coughed into his meaty hand and nodded at an empty chair off to the side, away from the long wooden table with The Devil's Deviants logo burned into the center. I'd always liked him. He was the type of man that would call you on your shit, without judgment, and then hold out his hand to help you up.

I nodded and sat, hoping that by the end of church everyone would forget about me. Watching and listening was the only way I was going to figure out where Stella was being held. The club didn't trust outsiders, and while nomads were still Deviants, I no longer belonged to a charter or got a vote. Which made me not only a traitor in their eyes but also an outsider.

Tweak threw his hands up in the air. "So, we're seriously just going to ignore the elephant in the room?"

There went my chance at blending in. Damn Tweak and his big fucking mouth. He was calling me out because he had mad love for Stella, and I respected that, but it still made me want to punch his pretty face in. Let's see how much pussy he got with a black eye and a missing tooth.

"Yes," Ryder huffed out with a glower. "I invited Switch to be a part of the recovery operation because Stella's going to need all the support she can get. Anyone have a problem with that?"

He stared down the table, daring anyone to speak up. When he was satisfied no one was going to say shit about me being here, he continued, "Good. Now, since this is Hunter's show, I'm turning it over to him."

Hunter cocked his head to the side, his cold eyes assessing me as he spoke. "Their pattern is to rotate the girls every couple of days until they're sold, and if I'm right, she's already been at that location for two days. If we don't grab her tonight, they'll move her, and I'll have to start all over again. We've found twenty safe houses so far, but I suspect there's more."

"Jesus Christ," Gunner muttered under his

breath as he pulled his shoulder length hair away from his face. "Has the boyfriend resurfaced yet?"

A boyfriend? Stella had a fucking boyfriend? The thought of another man touching my girl made me want to put my fist through the wall. Then again, what the hell did I think would happen? Anyone with eyes could tell underneath all the baggy coveralls she was fond of lay a body meant for sin.

I should have never listened when she was hurling angry words in my face. Worse yet, I'd stayed away. God, I was an idiot, and I had no one to blame but myself. Ryder had been right all along. She might have been off limits to the club, but not the rest of the men in the world.

Fuck, I needed a smoke if I was going to deal with this shit.

"No," Hunter deadpanned. "Unless his body magically turns up somewhere, I'll keep looking."

Tweak's eyes, dark as Ryder's, narrowed on his cousin. "What about the dude before him? The one I had a bad feeling about. Did you ever check into him?"

Jesus, there were two fuckers who'd had their grubby little hands on her. Two!

My hands balled into fists in my lap, my nails breaking through the skin of my palms. She'd had fewer boyfriends than that in high school. Of course, back then I'd been around to scare off even the most persistent of them. Might have even ended a guy's football career with a well-placed boot to his throwing arm. It wasn't my finest hour, but it was better than having to face this shit.

"Yes," Ryder said, bringing me back to the present. "Antonio Sanchez is dirty, but clean. He uses his legitimate businesses to keep up appearances like we do, only he sells guns instead of drugs. Trust me, he was the first person I suspected of being behind her abduction. I even had Colt following him around in the van for a few days after she went missing."

Colt spoke up from the end of the table. "He only left his house to go to the club, and both times he had the same security people with him and rode in the same car. His house has tons of staff coming and going at all hours of the day and night, including a stuffy doorman, so if he took her, it would be unlikely that he'd keep her there."

"What about his club?" I asked, figuring Tweak had already opened pandora's box.

He leaned forward, his spiky brown hair no longer blocked by Gunner's shoulder.

The first thing I noticed was the absence of a prominent prospect rocker from the front of his cut. Good for him. It had been a long time coming. The kid had never balked at anything that was asked of him, even when it meant getting his hands dirty.

"While I was waiting for him to finish his meeting, I had a look around. His club doesn't have a basement or rooftop access, and they left all the doors unlocked except for the manager's office. When I came up empty-handed after picking the lock, I asked Brandy to hack into his security system. All she could tell me for sure was that Stella hadn't been there in the last two days."

Ryder drummed his fingers against the table as he looked over at me. "See, dirty but clean."

"I hate to even think this," Beast interrupted, scrubbing a hand down his face. "But we haven't been able to get a visual. How do we know they haven't already sold her?"

"Because I'm currently the highest bidder."

Silence descended on the room at Hunter's statement. I sat forward, letting my hands dangle between my knees. "So, you know who these bastards are?"

Hunter had a stare that made you feel like a bug under a microscope, and even after all these years I still didn't have a clue what went on inside his head. Maybe I didn't want to. Something told me it wasn't the most pleasant place to be.

"Yes, and no. I've identified all the men coming and going from the warehouse where I believe she's being held, but not who they take their orders from. Whoever's behind this isn't some dumb, low-rent criminal. Their website has layers upon layers of security and it's masked to look like an antique furniture auction site. They've cleverly disguised the descriptions of the girls to match pieces of furniture. A mint condition mahogany rococo chiffonier would be code for a tall eighteen-year-old African American virgin. You need an invitation to view the girls' pictures and a passcode to bid."

Ryder ran a hand through his dark hair, leaving the ends sticking out in places. "And how did you warrant such an invitation?"

"Now, that's the million-dollar question, isn't it? Was it because someone was looking to capitalize on my ties to the *Braterstwo* or were they trying to send the club a message?"

Hunter's pale eyes found mine. "Stella may not be safe even after we get her back. Are you prepared to help me, even if it means following my orders, or are you going to become a liability I need to dispose of?"

He might be a cold psychotic bastard who was just as likely to kill you as he was to help you, but at least he was honest about it. I'd never heard of the Braterstwo, but if Hunter was involved with them, they weren't to be trifled with.

My enemies were starting to pile up, and I was no closer to getting Stella back than when I walked through that door. Fuck. It seemed for now, at least, I had no choice but to work with Hunter.

"I'll play by your rules as long as I'm the one who gets to kill the bastards."

"Funny you should mention that. Brandy made me promise that once Stella was clear, I'd kill them all." He shrugged. "She never specified that I had to be the one to slit their throats. Knock yourself out."

I still didn't know who in the hell Brandy was, but she'd just become my new favorite person.

CHAPTER 6

STELLA

My body felt like one giant bruise, the ground underneath me cold and unyielding. Where the fuck was I? There was a faint glow of light to the right, but my head hurt too much to bother turning toward it. Muted cries echoed off the walls, so it was probably a small mercy that I couldn't see a hand in front of my face.

A whisper of movement made me tense, and I immediately regretted it. My stomach rolled like it did whenever I got on a boat. I could almost feel the phantom waves rocking me. Weakness held my limbs in place, and I wondered if I was going to die choking on my vomit in wherever the hell this was.

"Don't move," a high-pitched male voice whispered.

Wait. I knew that voice. Everything was disjointed and slow inside my head as I tried to grasp on to the fleeting thought.

"They're monitoring us on the cameras, and I don't want them to know you're awake. They worked me over pretty good and with the drugs still floating around in your system we won't last a minute against them."

His voice quieted to a squeak when he spoke again, and I had to strain to hear him.

"Get some sleep. I'll wake you up when it's time to get the hell out of here."

Yes. That sounded sensible. Sleep, then I would leave this place. My body settled and darkness once again enveloped me. Only this darkness wasn't absolute. It came with haunting dreams of a man with cinnamon-colored eyes.

∽✕✤✕∼

The stands were packed with students, all of them cheering for Derek, our star quarterback. He was agile as he faked right, then left, before he reached back to throw the ball. Another player hit his arm right as he launched it, the spiral more wobbly than tight. Everyone turned their heads downfield, but my gaze never left Derek. His body remained suspended in the air before it plummeted back down to Earth. His back touched the turf a second before his helmet, several players falling on top of him.

I held my breath, the screams of the kids jumping on the bleachers letting me know the ball had made it into the end zone. The roar was deafening. Thanks to Derek Hughes's arm we'd just won state. He'd done what he'd set out to do, impress the scouts that were sitting somewhere in the stands.

Whistles blew, and players started helping other players to their feet. At the bottom of the pile was Derek, lying there, not moving. Oh, god. Was he hurt? My lungs froze as pandemonium continued going on all around me. Did these fuckers not care? What the hell was the matter with them?

Suddenly, Derek sat up and lifted his helmet off his head. He stared into the stands until his dark blue eyes landed on me. Butterflies took flight in my stomach as he lifted his helmet up in victory and winked at me.

He didn't know it yet, but he was going to be mine. At least for tonight. Fuck Switch and his long, beautiful, thickly veined cock. I wouldn't fuck that asshole now if he begged me to. But I would rub it in his face that I'd fucked Derek. He might even get a text of my hand wrapped around Derek's cock. Unless it was tiny, then I'd just brag.

It was the least he deserved for giving that bitch Mona a ride home on the back of his bike. Again.

Smoke practically came out of my ears when I remembered having to listen to her brag to Betty Sue about him bending her over his bike in chemistry class. It made me want to take a Bunsen burner to her precious flowing locks until Betty Sue let it slip that Mona had a crush on Derek. Two birds, one stone, and all that happy horseshit.

Was revenge dick a little petty? Absolutely. Was I going to let that stop me? Hell no. If Switch had it his way, I'd die a virgin while he dipped his dick in any old hole he pleased. Well, two could play that game. Not that I planned to go all slutzilla or anything, but there was no harm in seeing what all the fuss was about.

Speaking of that, everyone was exiting the bleachers and if I didn't hightail it down to the locker rooms, I'd miss Derek when he came out. Damn it. There was a sea of bodies pressed together and a lot of steps to the bottom. This wouldn't do at all. I stared over the side of the railing and gauged if I could make the drop. Nope, better go halfway down first.

There were a few advantages to being skinny and having a resting bitch face. Sure, I got the oddball look, or the occasional outraged huff, but everyone let me squeeze by them. When I reached the halfway point, I jumped over the railing with a grin, listening to a lady scream as I fell.

My boots touched the pavement, and I stood, my hands cupping my mouth to holler back up at her. "Sorry!"

She looked down at me like I was a lunatic instead of just a line cutter, but I didn't give a fuck. I had bigger fish to fry and a virginity to lose. Which was why I jogged my happy ass in the opposite direction of the crowd. It was easier to go all the way around the stadium than it was to fight my way through.

Bushes lined the outside of the stadium, and I stuck close to them, keeping away from the vast pools of light cast by the spotlights above. There was a seldomly used pathway on this side that led directly to the underground locker rooms. My boots echoed off the sloping pavement as I made my way into the bowels of the stadium.

The scrape of another set of boots let me know I wasn't alone. A second later, I was being lifted off my feet and slammed against the cement wall. The scent of leather, citrus, and tobacco gave away who had me long before I saw the outline of his face.

My traitorous body rejoiced in the contact, and I wished I could say his manhandling didn't make my panties wet. But whenever he was around, I had a nasty habit of thinking with my pussy and not my brain.

"Why the fuck are you back here. Alone. In the dark." His words were like venom, but I loved the sting. "Do you have any idea how dangerous that is?"

He was too close. With every breath I took, his arm brushed against my nipple. Who the hell had I been kidding? I'd still fuck the shit out of him. All he had to do was ask. We both knew he wasn't going to, but that didn't keep me from wanting him to. And there it was, my weakness. Switch was the bane of my existence and in this moment that pissed me off like nothing else could.

"Let me go." I shoved against his chest with all my might, but he didn't step back. Not an inch. "I have a hot date waiting for me in the tunnel."

He flinched as if I'd slapped him. But that couldn't be right. He saw me as one of the guys. A friend like Ryder. A buddy. Pfft. The only time that word should be used was when fuck came before it.

"Derek," he snarled like his very name offended him.

"Yeah. What's it to you?"

He edged even closer, his jean clad leg slipping between mine. Holy fuck, but did I want to ride his leg like a shameless and desperate whore. For him, I guess I was. The dark concealed his profile, and I wished I could see his eyes. Cinnamon-colored eyes that heated my skin like a brand.

"Mad Dog wouldn't like you going out with him."

There it was. His convenient excuse. My father. He was a broken record that I'd grown tired of listening to.

"Mad Dog or you," I shot back at him, struggling in his hold.

All it got me was aching nipples and a slick thong.

"Ahh," I screamed into the night, determined to

fight him.

Fuck him and my pussy too! They were both assholes for doing this to me.

"It doesn't matter. Derek will be recovering from an unfortunate accident for the foreseeable future. He really should have been more careful."

He bared his teeth as he spit the words, and I knew he'd done something awful. Remorse, shame, hell, even pity for the man who should have been my first would have been normal. I felt none of those things. The wetness pooling between my thighs was all I could focus on. All I could think about.

His mouth descended on mine as his hand tangled in the long strands of my hair. It was wild and desperate. Teeth clashed and tongues stroked. My body felt like it was burning from the inside out and I couldn't get enough. This. This was what poets wrote sonnets about, what crooners sang songs about.

And before I knew it, it was over. He backed away slowly, stepping into a pool of light as he went. His chest heaved beneath his plain white T-shirt, a tremor snaking its way down his lean frame as he gave me one last lingering look before he melted into the darkness.

CHAPTER 7

STELLA

Drip, drip, drip. The scuffling of feet from somewhere far away echoed back to me. Drip, drip, drip. A whimper came from somewhere close by. Drip, drip, drip. Hazy memories played like a highlight reel behind my eyelids as I listened. Drip, drip, drip. My fingers twitched, the pads lightly tracing over a cool, hard surface. A sniffle came from the same direction as the whimper. Drip, drip, drip.

Jesus. Where in the hell was I? My eyelashes stuck together when I tried to open my eyes, and my mouth felt dry and gross. Funny, I didn't remember having anything to drink at the club.

The club. Shit. Everything came rushing back in stark clarity and I instantly shot upright.

Bad move. My head swam, and I tried to blink away the overlapping metal bars that danced in front of me. Fuck. My stomach lurched, and I quickly squeezed my eyes shut.

Whatever that asshole had shot me with packed a hell of a punch. After taking several deep breaths in, then back out again, the nausea finally subsided, and I was able to open my eyes.

Dim light filtered through the single set of bars on my cell. Let me amend that, jail cell, since this was some shit straight out of *Locked Up*. Only way worse.

A shiver slid down my spine as I stared at the mattress lying atop the concrete floor. There wasn't enough light for me to be sure, but I suspected the dark stains were dried blood. Gross.

Nope. Not going to go there. Thinking about it wouldn't help me escape from this shithole. I shook my head and forced myself not to dwell on the mattress from hell.

On the opposite wall was a cracked sink, a stained toilet with no toilet paper, and Jules folded up in the corner next to it.

Holy shit. Had they really been dumb enough to put us in a cell together, or was this some kind of sick joke?

His head was bent at an awkward angle

with his chin almost touching his shoulder. He was curled into a tight little ball, his long arms draped over his knees. With the dim lighting, it was difficult for me to tell if he was just asleep or dead. Fuck me, I hoped he wasn't dead.

"Psst, Jules. Are you okay over there?"

When he didn't move, I blew out a breath and scooted closer. The tiny dress I wore hampered my movements, but I was too relieved that I still had it on to care.

"Jules," I whispered.

Nothing. Fantastic. There was no way around it, I was going to have to feel for a pulse. If he was gone, well shit, I'd just cross that bridge when I came to it.

Loose pebbles from the cement floor dug into my knees as I carefully leaned over his body and placed two fingers against the side of his neck. When I encountered warm, firm skin, I let out the breath I'd been holding. Not dead. At least not yet.

"Don't move your hand and lean in," he whispered. The hairs on the back of my neck stood up, but I did as he asked. "We haven't got much time. When the men come in here, shrink into the opposite corner and tell them I'm dead. While they're distracted, run as fast as you can down the hall and take a right at the fork. It's a straight shot to the outer door from there."

"What about you?" I asked, careful not to move my hand away from his neck.

A memory of Jules's squeaky voice warning me about cameras surfaced, and I tried to hide my shiver. The thought of someone watching me while I was passed out freaked me the fuck out. My brain refused to think about anything worse happening to me while I was in that state.

"I'm sorry." There it was again. The same thing he'd said at the club when those assholes took us. "You were the only one who could lead me to them. My last shot at finding my sister. Remember what I told you. One turn and you're free."

Footsteps echoed as they drew closer, and I scurried to the opposite side of the cell, curling myself into a ball. It wasn't hard to fake tears. Lava pooled in my gut and for once in my life I didn't have to hide them. Being tough was a disadvantage here. I needed these men to think of me as being weak and helpless.

Keys rattled in the lock, and when the door swung open, I looked up at them through my lashes. There was something oddly familiar about the jawline of the man who stood over me, but I couldn't place where I'd seen him before. Not that it mattered. He and I were about to part company.

"He's"—I sucked in a shaky breath for this douche's benefit—"dead."

The man turned, a swath of light landing on his blue-black hair. Something gnawed at me, but I remained still, waiting for him to move away. His back was well defined, the muscles bunching under his black fitted T-shirt as he moved.

He reminded me of Hunter, not a large man in stature, but still deadly and powerful. I had to time this just right if I stood a chance of escaping.

He left our cell door open as he walked over to where Jules sat, still curled up in his unmoving ball. When he went down on his haunches and extended his hand toward Jules's neck to check for a pulse, I sprang into action. His shoulders tensed at the sound of movement behind him, but he didn't stop me as I ran out the door.

Maybe he thought I wouldn't be able to find my way out of this hellhole or that I'd give up when I came across more guards. Wrong on both counts, asshole. I had no intention of sticking around to see what sort of horrors they had in store for me.

Cells lined both sides of the wide hallway and my heart thudded in my ears as I ran, careful not to look in any of them as I passed. If I didn't make it out, I wouldn't be able to help myself let alone anyone else.

I made myself a promise, though. As soon as I was in the clear, I'd come back and free any women imprisoned here before I rained down hell on the entire place. All of it would be nothing but rubble and ash by the time I was done, the men's bodies burning in the very cells they had used.

My bare feet slapped against the cement as I ran, the sound echoing down the hall behind me. When I reached the fork, just like Jules said, I slowed down just enough to make the turn.

Only, I didn't see the arm stretched out in front of me until it was colliding with my chest. My body jerked with the force of the hit, and there was nothing I could do to stop myself from falling backward. The last thing I saw before everything went black was the same handsome angel who'd stuck me with a needle back at Antonio's club.

CHAPTER 8

STELLA

There was no doubt about it, I'd had my bell rung. My head had its own heartbeat and pain radiated from what I felt sure was a sizable lump at the back of my head. But I was alive, and as long as my heart was still beating, I'd fight these assholes every step of the way. If for no other reason than to make them regret taking me.

When I opened my eyes, I was staring up at the same ceiling. Fuck. I was right back where I'd started, and judging by the stiff material touching my skin I was lying atop the mattress from hell.

Cool air brushed against my skin like a caress, raising the hair on my arms and pebbling my nipples. Wait a second. When that fucker clotheslined me, I'd still had on my dress from the club.

Frantically, my hands moved along the front of my body only to find bare skin. I sat up, fighting the nausea that once again swamped me, using my hands to cover my tits and pussy as best as I could.

"Motherfucker!"

A male chuckle came from the darkened corner where Jules had been. "You won't be needing the dress anymore."

"Fuck you," I spat back, trying to put as much bravado as I could behind my words, given the situation.

He had the upper hand here, and we both knew it, but he'd never have the satisfaction of seeing me cower. Once men like him caught a whiff of fear, you were as good as dead.

If I stood any chance of surviving, I'd have to be smart, bide my time, and be ready when the opportunity presented itself. Because I planned on living long enough to see these men pay.

"So much spark," he purred. "We'll have to see what we can do to change that."

His words had hit their mark. Fear slid down my spine like a serpent, leaving me cold, thinking of all the ways he'd try to break me. Outwardly, however, I sat up straighter and raised an eyebrow.

"Bring him in."

His voice was smooth, with no discernible accent to give away where he was from. I racked my brain trying to think if I'd ever heard it before, but I was coming up blank.

The cell door opened, and the handsome douche who'd clotheslined me during my brief escape attempt shoved Jules inside and forced him to his knees.

He might have had the face of an angel, but it was only a carefully crafted illusion to hide the demon that lurked beneath his pretty face. It was a dangerous combination, one that I was sure had tricked many girls. Just not me.

His tongue traced his bottom lip as he let his eyes roam over the parts of my body not covered by my hands and I bared my teeth at him.

Another chuckle came from the darkened corner. "She's glorious, no? When I saw her, I knew she'd make an excellent addition to someone's collection."

He'd just confirmed my earlier suspicion that I had seen him somewhere before. But where? We must not have spoken because if we had I would have remembered his voice.

"Fuck you. I'm no man's pet."

The handsome demon chuckled. "Boss, you're going to have your work cut out for you with this one. But you're right, she'll fetch a pretty penny."

Finally, it dawned on me what these men were. Human traffickers. The scum of the earth, selling women like cattle.

My eyes narrowed and I spit at the handsome demon with what little I had in my overly dry mouth. Fuck them. I'd bite the cock off any man that came near me.

His eyes flashed at the spit that landed near his boot and took a step toward me, his hand raised. My chin jutted in the air, ready to take the punch. This wouldn't be the first time a man laid his hands on me. The last one wound up six feet under, and this one would eventually face the same fate. I'd make sure of it, even if it was the last thing I ever did.

"Tut, tut, tut, Michael." Hatred burned bright in his eyes at having been called off by someone higher up the food chain than him. "You know we can't sell damaged goods, and I'm looking forward to proving that The Devil's Deviants aren't nearly as untouchable as they think they are."

What he said didn't make any sense. Everything pointed to Antonio's enemies being responsible. I'd been shot at in front of his house and then taken from his club. Even selling me into sexual slavery would have been more of a slap in Antonio's face than my father's.

If this was about the club, and Antonio had nothing to do with it, then why had they taken me? My father was a founding member, sure, but he'd given up his VP spot years ago. He was only a member now, which was the lowest man on the totem pole. They would get more bang for their buck by taking Ryder's old lady, Valentina, or I swallowed, even Hunter's old lady, Brandy.

My gut told me not to take anything this man said at face value. Despite them alluding to me pulling in a pretty penny, I doubted money was the motivating factor in their decision to sell me. They could have easily killed me, and it would have sent the same message.

No, something here stank like yesterday's trash, and I needed to figure out what in the hell was going on before anyone I loved got hurt. Looked as though I was going to be stuck, naked, in this hellhole with these assholes for the foreseeable future.

That didn't mean I was going to play nice. I'd die before I ever let them break me. Hopefully, by the time they figured that out I'd have the answers I needed.

"What makes you think they'd even care about some old timer's daughter?"

One nod of his dark head and Michael pressed the muzzle of his gun against Jules's temple. Fuck, I had forgotten he was even here.

"What was the name of the young man you gave me? The one that I believe you said, and I quote, watches her like a hawk?"

Michael pressed the muzzle of his gun hard enough against Jules's temple to move his head a fraction of an inch and Jules hissed, "Tweak."

Laughter bubbled out of me, and I was having a hard time keeping my hands in place. Really? These assholes were not only cruel, but dumb as a box of rocks. No wonder they took me. They knew fuck all about the club, otherwise they'd have known that Tweak was a man whore.

"What is it you find so amusing?"

He sounded pissed. Good. That's what he got for throwing me in a cell, letting his douche lackey clothesline me, and stripping off my dress while I was passed out. I shouldn't even bother to clue his ass in about Tweak, but I wanted to see what he'd do with the information. That and if he recognized Antonio's name.

"Hate to break this to you"—I paused and gave him a fake-ass smile—"whatever your name is. I'm afraid I was too busy running out the cell door to ask the name of my captor."

"Mateo," he said through clenched teeth.

"Mateo," I repeated, drawing out the O just to annoy him. "Tweak will fuck any girl with a pulse and a penchant for costumes. The club won't have a clue that this attack wasn't directed at my boyfriend Antonio Sanchez. Maybe you've heard of him."

"Hmm, indeed I have." His face was half in shadow, so it was difficult to read him. "It seems I have no use for Jules then." The gun went off, making me jump, and Jules's body fell forward.

"Let's talk again in a few days and see if you're feeling less combative."

My teeth chattered, and not from the chill in the air. I watched both men walk out of the cell because looking down at what was left of Jules's head, or the blood splattered across my naked body, wasn't an option. They didn't deserve to hear me scream. Not now, not ever.

"W…w…wait!"

The cell door slammed shut, the finality of the metal lock echoing off the walls. My captor, Mateo, glared back at me. His gray eyes would have been arresting had they not held such loathing.

"Yes, little one?"

"You can't just leave a dead body in here!" I hated the note of desperation in my tone, but it wasn't every day a man was shot in front of me and dumped at my feet.

He smiled, but it held no warmth. "You got him killed, now you can clean up the mess."

CHAPTER 9

SWITCH

When church was over, I expected Ryder to stay behind and give me shit about being ready to move out tonight, but he'd cleared out along with everybody else. Well, almost everybody. The last person I wanted to talk to right now stood in front of my chair, preventing me from leaving.

Mad Dog still had a commanding presence, despite his graying beard and weathered face. Maybe it was because the mantle of responsibility still clung to him like a shroud long after he'd been forced to give up his title.

Carpal tunnel may have taken away his ability to ride for long periods of time or fire a weapon, but it could never diminish the fierceness with which he protected his club and his daughter.

His brows drew together as he stroked a beard that had gotten shorter and shorter over the last couple of years. "Glad to see you looking like shit."

Thanks for that, captain obvious. Apparently, everybody and their brother felt the need to comment on my appearance today. Yeah. I looked like a bag of ass. Check.

"If that's all," I said as I stood, too hungover to entertain any bullshit remarks.

He never stepped back, putting us toe to toe. "No, that ain't all."

If it had been anyone else, I would have told them to fuck off because I had no interest in rehashing old history. But it wasn't. He was Stella's old man, a senior club member, and a man I'd respected since the day I learned what in the hell that word meant.

He wanted to sort our shit out now, so be it. I'd give him his due, but it would have to be quick. We only had four hours before we rode out, and I desperately needed a cigarette, Tylenol, and a bed. In that order.

"We're short on time, so say what you gotta say."

"Fine. You not only let Stella fuck with your head, but then you went and let your feelings cloud your judgment." Shit, I was already regretting my decision, and he was just getting started. "That fuckup almost got everyone here killed, Stella included."

"Bullshit."

The old man was stretching things a bit. My abandoning the club when they needed me wasn't in question, nor were the consequences of those actions for the men I had called brothers. They had a right to hate me, not that I could or would take back what I had done. What I failed to see was how the violence would have spilled over onto Stella.

"I can't decide if you've been lying to yourself all this time or you're really that stupid. Did Miguel strike you as the type of man who had an aversion to killing women or a history of leaving survivors? What did you think, he'd slaughter the club and then let Stella work in the shop? A shop that, I might add, he had no use for. Boy, use your damn head."

Damn. He was right, and I'd been too busy licking my wounds to see it. Miguel was a nasty piece of work. If he'd risk killing his own daughter just for a shot at controlling the drug trade in the US, why in the hell would he let Stel live.

I'd put her in danger twice by leaving. The first time I'd been lucky Hunter was there to clean up my mess. This time, I was going to have to face the consequences of my actions.

"I see from the look on your face that you've finally gotten your head out of your ass. For Stella's sake, I intend to make sure it stays that way."

"Don't get in my way, old man," I snarled, pointing a finger at his chest.

He was right, damn him, but that didn't mean I was going to let him come between me and Stel. Not anymore. She was mine, and I was staying no matter what he or anybody else had to say about it.

"I have more love for you than I ever did for my old man, but I'm done pussyfooting around my feelings for Stel out of respect for you. When we get her back, and we will or I'll die trying, I'm never leaving her again. No matter what she says."

"Is that what all this back-and-forth bullshit has been about? Stella's been running her own love life since she was sixteen because lord knows I don't need her in mine." He shivered. "The first time she tried to tell me who I could fuck we'd be coming to blows."

"Are you fucking shitting me right now?"

All this time I could have been balls deep in Stel! He wasn't serious. He couldn't be serious. It was too cruel. Any second someone was going to pop out and say gotcha. Either that or he was going to clock me for wanting to fuck Stel. Not that I blamed him.

He grinned. "Lucky for you, she got her

momma's shitty taste in men. Once she decides on you, there's no changing her mind, no matter how bad you fuck up."

His smile fell as his hands settled on his hips. "But she's also proud, stubborn, strongwilled, and fiery. Stella is going to try your patience and be hell to live with, just like her old man."

I'd been obsessively studying Stel since the sixth grade. He wasn't telling me anything I didn't already know. Fuck. I couldn't decide if I wanted to punch something, hug him, or both.

"Now, go get some sleep, and for fuck's sake, clean yourself up."

He didn't need to tell me twice. The second he moved to the side enough for me to squeeze past him, I headed for the door.

"And Switch?"

"Yeah," I said, looking over my shoulder to meet an intense pair of light blue eyes.

"If you ever leave her again, or break her heart, I'll shoot you in the nuts. Understood?"

For the first time since Stel told me to fuck off all those months ago, the tightness in my chest eased a fraction. We weren't out of the woods yet, and a million and one things could still go wrong, but at least I had one less obstacle to face when I got my girl back. And I would.

Somehow, someway, she'd find her way back to me. Then I'd make her mine in every sense of the word.

"I'll save you the trouble and let Stel do it."

His laughter followed me all the way out the door.

◦◦◦

A brush of cool air made the shower curtain flutter, and I stilled. The sound of water splashing against the tiles masked my step back. My gun was on the back of the toilet, only an arm's length away. It would have to be enough. Using the gap between the curtain and the tile, I looked into the mirror, trying to catch a glimpse of whoever was trying to get the drop on me.

The breath I'd been holding left my chest in a whoosh when I caught sight of her standing in the doorway. She shifted her weight from foot to foot as she bit the corner of her nail.

Fuck. Stel couldn't be in here when I was in the shower. How in the hell was I supposed to control myself when all I wanted to do was tug her into the shower with me and tear off every stitch of clothing she had on.

A groan broke free before I could help it. I thought for sure it would send her running out the door. But no, not her. There wasn't a meek bone in Stel's body, and she'd set her sights on me. Resisting her was making me fucking crazy, not to mention hard all the damn time.

Maybe if she thought I was jacking off, she'd leave me to it. Hell, I was already hard knowing she was in the bathroom with me, and in my experience,

72

a Stel induced hard-on didn't just disappear with thoughts of little old ladies and fuzzy bunnies.

I gripped the base of my dick, wishing it was her petite hand wrapped around me, and slid my hand along my length to the tip.

"Fuck."

Her beautiful honey-colored eyes widened as she sucked in a breath, her chest expanding. God those tits. What I wouldn't give to see them without the black tank top. To bury my face in them and inhale a whiff of vanilla mixed with the paint from the car she'd been working on earlier.

My hand lost its rhythm for a second as I pictured using my teeth to tease her nipples into tight peaks before I sucked the hard buds into my mouth. Another strangled groan left my lips as she shifted to the side and slid her hand into the front of the baggy jeans she wore.

This girl was going to be the death of me. Literally. Mad Dog was going to gut me for wanting to defile his baby girl. But I couldn't help it. When I closed my eyes at night, I saw her on her hands and knees before me, her round ass begging for my handprint, and her pussy dripping for my cock.

She let out a breathy little moan that was almost my undoing, but I wanted to watch her come. I needed for her to come while we breathed the same air, to know she thought of me while she did it, because that was as close as I would ever get to fucking her. To having her the way I wanted.

The waistband of her jeans slid down with the

motion of her hand, revealing the thin red strap clinging to her hipbone. Fuck me. She was wearing a red thong. My favorite. The fact she didn't even know it was my favorite made it all the sweeter.

Her long, silky wave of blond hair brushed her arm as she tilted her head back. Her pale pink lips parted on a gasp as she came. I thought her rage was the most beautiful thing I'd ever seen. I was wrong. Stella in the throes of an orgasm was like Beethoven's symphony or Michelangelo's art, sheer unadulterated perfection.

Then I let go, painting the gray checkered shower curtain a milky white. Only I didn't shout her name the way I'd wanted to. No, I had a dream to kill. She could never know about my obsession. I needed to be a dick in order to keep her at arm's length. So, I shouted a name we both hated, but for different reasons. Mona.

Looking at her face as she froze, her hand still in the front of her jeans, killed me. But I made myself do it. Made myself take her pain as well as my own.

She didn't scream or charge the curtain. It would have been better if she had. Maybe if she'd punched me a few times for good measure, I'd be able to breathe.

No. Instead, she removed her hand from her jeans and looked down at it in disgust. That was a stab in the heart, not that I didn't deserve it. Then she slowly backed away without making a sound. Another piece of my heart shattered, but it didn't matter. It had only ever beat for her, anyway.

My eyelids fluttered open, a soft buzzing sound coming from beside my head. Fuck. How long had I been out for?

I looked over at the illuminated screen on my burner phone and saw I had a message. Sitting up, I ran a hand over my face and reached for the pack of cigarettes on the nightstand. This was the first time in a long time that I'd woken up halfway sober.

For Stel, I was going to have to go cold turkey. She needed the old me, and not some broken down train wreck.

My phone beeped again, and I lit my cigarette, a slight tremor in my hand as I reached for it.

Hunter: Time to collect the package.

CHAPTER 10

STELLA

It had been a few days since my captor made good on his promise and left me alone with Jules's dead body. Somehow, the horror of my situation seemed less daunting if I pretended that he was a rambunctious spirit like in *Beetlejuice*. Not sure what it said about my mental state that I spoke to a corpse, but that was a problem for future Stella. This Stella only cared about holding in her screams.

"Are you okay over there," a girl whispered.

Her voice had a creepy echo to it that reverberated off the walls to my right. This was the first time anyone had spoken to me since my captor left. At least, I assumed she was talking to me since Jules wasn't long on conversation these days.

"I'm just peachy, but Jules could stand a breath mint," I snarked back from my spot atop the mattress from hell. Guess I wasn't much for chit chat these days either.

"Jolene," another girl hissed from farther away. "What are you doing? Shut up. She already got her boyfriend killed. Do you really want to be next?"

"Calm your tits," I muttered, trying to shift into a more comfortable position while still keeping my parts covered with my hands. "He wasn't my boyfriend."

"What was he doing in there with you then if he wasn't your boyfriend?"

For a second, I debated about how much I should reveal in case anyone was listening. Then I remembered it didn't really matter what I said. They already knew Antonio was my boyfriend, Jules was dead, and unless I got to talk to these assholes again, none of us were getting out of here.

"He worked for the guy I was…" I stopped short. Antonio and I weren't serious, yet fucking, while accurate, made me seem slutty, so that description was out. Finally, I settled for, "Seeing."

"He was like a driver or something?"

Jolene reminded me of Cherry, and a wave of homesickness hit me like a freight train. What I wouldn't give for a taste of her sunshine right about now, even if she annoyed the shit out of me with her perkiness.

"He was her bodyguard you idiot," the other girl shot back.

"Some job he did. She's in here the same as us."

Jolene had a point. My eyes strayed to Jules's back even though I willed them to look anywhere but at him. Memories from the night we were taken came flooding back as I stared at the visual reminder of my nightmare. Every detail of that night, at least until the drugs took effect, was burned into my brain.

His words, though, were what haunted me the most. 'I'm sorry, Stella. I had no other choice.' What the hell did that even mean?

Then suddenly all the pieces began to fall into place, and I couldn't believe I hadn't figured it out before now. He'd gotten us captured on purpose.

"That asshole!"

Hazy memories surfaced from the depths of my subconscious and took shape. The crunch of gravel under tires. A muted grunt followed by the rattling of chains. Lights flickering from above before I felt the chill of a hard surface. A familiar voice in the darkness letting me know he'd wake me when it was time to leave.

"Which one?" the girl asked, bringing me back to the present.

"The one who got me thrown in here."

My voice sounded small, almost far away, and I wasn't sure she'd even heard me until I heard her mirthless chuckle.

"Don't be too hard on yourself. He fooled me too, and I'm not one to be swayed by a pretty face."

She had to be referring to the douche who drugged and clotheslined me because Jules wasn't handsome. At least not in the classical sense. Brutally arresting, maybe. Tall, dark, and dangerous with an air of competency, absolutely. Not that I thought Jules made it a habit of screwing women over. No, that privilege was all mine.

And for what? They'd killed him within the first twenty-four hours because he had nothing on the club. Maybe, like me, he'd assumed this was about Antonio. Then he might have had a bargaining chip or two. It fit, but it was still a hell of a gamble. Whatever he'd been after, he'd been willing to die for it.

Damn my survival instincts. Once I knew I was on my own, I'd zeroed in on his instructions. The rest hadn't mattered at the time. Now, I knew the things I'd dismissed held the key to what got me thrown into this hellhole to begin with. Think, Stella, think. What did he say?

Jesus. Why couldn't I remember? Every

minute detail about being taken was crystal clear in my mind, and yet I couldn't seem to remember a few measly sentences he uttered right before my failed escape attempt. Maybe that douche had knocked a screw loose with his wrestling moves.

The heavy clomp of boots echoed down the corridor and a hush fell over us. Even I held my breath, waiting to see what new hell awaited me. The last time I'd had visitors in my cell they left a dead body.

Shiny black combat boots stopped at the door of my cell, and I looked up. Wow, the saying really was true, speak of the devil and he shall appear. It was a shame that a douche like Michael came in such an angelic package. He'd probably tricked the girl I'd spoken to, and that made me hate him all the more.

He unlocked my cell door, the hinges groaning in protest as he swung it open. "Come on killer. You're about to be somebody else's headache."

"What do you mean?"

My eyes searched his face, hoping he'd give me some sort of a clue if this was par for the course or a bad sign. His eyes traveled down to the hand covering my tits and back up to my face. He might as well have been inspecting cattle for all the emotion he showed.

"Time for you to be broken in." His eyes dropped back down to the hand covering the top of my mound. "Who knows? Maybe I'll have the pleasure of hearing you scream in the next rotation."

CHAPTER 11

STELLA

We emerged from an old barn cellar just as the sun was sinking below the horizon. A small grouping of trees dotted the landscape in the distance, breaking up the grassy fields that surrounded us.

My stomach did an uncomfortable somersault when I realized that even if I had gotten past Michael earlier, I wouldn't have made it very far. There was nothing but open countryside as far as the eye could see. They'd have caught up with me long before I found the road out of this hellhole.

Michael prodded me along like cattle, literally, cutting off my internal pity party. Naked and chained, I shuffled toward the two assholes casually leaning against a white delivery van parked a few feet away. How utterly typical of them. If I weren't so preoccupied with hiding my goodies, or the damn cattle prod grazing my skin that could become electrified at any moment, I might be tempted to ask these two bozos where they hid the candy and puppies.

My eyes scanned the waiting men as we moved closer, committing every detail about them to memory. Good thing neither would be hard to pick out of a crowd. One of them had a dragon tattoo on his neck done in vibrant oranges and reds, while the other had a shock of bright red hair braided down the middle of his head.

Mateo really should hire less conspicuous muscle if he wanted to keep his little flesh trade business going.

"What are you looking at?" the one with the neck tattoo asked.

Michael pulled me to a stop at the van door, his fingers biting into my flesh. "Be careful with this one. She's feisty."

He didn't know the half of it. If the playing field were a little more even, he'd be on the ground holding his balls right now. But no, the big dangerous man needed chains and a cattle prod to keep little old me in line. What a pathetic sack of human flesh.

Then there was Carrot Top off to the left, taking his time looking me over, his heavy-lidded gaze making my skin crawl. Not that I'd ever let him, or any of the rest of these jokers, know they had any effect on me. So, I lifted my chin a fraction as I glared back.

"You know I like the ones who haven't realized they're completely fucked yet."

"Yeah," Tattoo Neck added. "Once Boris is done with them, they're never the same. It sucks all the fun out of it for the rest of us."

Michael chuckled as he shoved me face first into the van. "Damn. I better catch up to her on the next rotation then, otherwise I'll miss out on all the fun."

Before any of those assholes had the chance to lay a finger on me, I squirmed the rest of the way into the van and rolled onto my side facing the door. There was no way I was staying ass up around these clowns. If they were planning on trying anything, I wanted to see it coming. But Michael only looked over and winked at me before he slid the van door shut, encasing me in darkness. How I hated that fucktwat.

The murmur of their voices moved away from the door, and I hurriedly rocked my shoulders back and forth against the soft shag carpeting that covered the floor of the van. When my head bumped into the passenger seat, I contorted my body to the side and groped around underneath it. I was trying to find something, anything, that I might use later to defend myself.

All I felt, though, was carpet. Disappointed, but not willing to give up yet, I scooted down until I felt the metal base of the driver's seat. My hand stretched, nothing but soft carpeting meeting the pads of my fingertips.

The voices outside became louder as the men rounded the front of the van, and frantically I slid my hand back and forth over the carpet. Right when I was about to admit defeat, I felt it.

A loose screw wasn't exactly the weapon I'd been hoping for, but I closed my hand around it anyway, and slid back into place just as the passenger door swung open.

Light filled the van, and it rocked as Tattoo Neck slid inside, looking over his shoulder at me. "Be a good girl and maybe I'll wait to take you to Boris."

Carrot Top opened the other door midway through his sentence and looked over at his partner. He shook his head as he sat down and closed the door, encasing us in darkness once again.

"Man, I thought you'd learned your lesson after the last girl we dropped off," he grumbled, starting the van.

The lights in the dash illuminated half of Tattoo Neck's face as he spoke. "I like to live dangerously. Besides, watching this one become a hollow shell feels like such a waste. What do you want to bet she's a hellcat in the sack?"

Carrot Top blew out a breath. "You're probably right, but the boss has a hard-on for this one. You want to take a chance on pissing him off?"

The leather seat squeaked as Tattoo Neck turned to face the front. "Not really."

"Didn't think so. Shame or not, we're taking her directly to Boris."

From the sound of things, I needed to be on my A game with Boris. Since they no longer seemed inclined to stop the van to fuck with me, I shut my eyes and tried to get some rest. Something told me it might be a long time before I had the chance again.

⁓⦵⦵⁓

The van's door slid open, jerking me awake. Bright light hit me square in the face, blinding me, my chains rattling as I lifted a hand up to shield my eyes. Someone stepped in front of the door, blocking all the light, their shadow swallowing me whole.

I blinked to clear the spots from my eyes and tilted my head back to have a look at the newest asshole. Big mistake. A shiver of dread worked its way down my spine as I gazed into the darkest, coldest eyes I'd ever seen. This had to be the Boris I'd heard so much about.

"I think you missed your calling," I snarked.

The slight tremor I couldn't keep out of my voice took away from the badass image I was going for, but I couldn't help it. He freaked me out in a way no one else ever had.

"Is that so?"

His calm velvety voice echoed back to me, almost making me lose my nerve. Unlike my old friend, Michael, this man's cruelty wasn't hidden beneath a mask of beauty. No, it was out there for all the world to see. He was literally a giant, walking, talking warning label for women everywhere.

"All you'd have to do is paint yourself green and you could be a body double for the *Jolly Green Giant*. The royalties from public appearances alone would be astronomical."

He lifted a brow, making his already elongated head look like something *Picasso* might have painted. The muscles in his thick neck bulged, a popping noise making me wince as he turned his neck first one way and then the other.

"Let's see how jolly you think I am, or how smart that mouth of yours is, after spending a few days with me."

Tattoo Neck stepped forward and jerked on my chains. My body slid, the rug rubbing the sensitive skin along the left side of my stomach. Boris smiled down at me before moving over to make room for Tattoo Neck to pull me from the van.

Damn. Why didn't he stick with the deadened stare? Even a deranged clown with his face painted into a wide grin while holding a bloody ax would have been preferable to his smile.

"I can get out on my own, thank you," I hissed at Tattoo Neck as I struggled to sit up.

He looked over at Boris, and when Boris nodded, Tattoo Neck let go of my chains and stalked off. I wish I could say I felt relieved to find myself with one less asshole to contend with, but I'd take him over the giant in front of me any day.

Shielding my eyes from the glaring light coming from the roofline above, I surveyed my newest prison. Mostly, so I wouldn't have to look at Boris because every time I did, it became harder to breathe.

Men with machine guns walked the perimeter of the massive gray metal building in front of me. Empty wooden pallets were stacked up next to a forklift on my left, and to my right sat a red semi-truck hitched up to a white trailer. Two Dobermans paced nervously in front of a plain black metal door, the sound of their chains grinding against the pavement making goose bumps break out along my flesh.

Boris spun on his heel and headed for the door. He expected me to follow him, but I stood there. Frozen. My earlier bravado was gone. All thoughts of needing to keep my family safe, gone. The only thing I could focus on was the feeling of dread that had invaded my system like a sickness.

Nobody needed to tell me terrible things happened here. You could feel the inky black cloud of evil clinging to the building like a vine.

Misery had held my previous hellhole in its tight grip, but it was nothing like this. I wasn't foolish enough to think that bad things hadn't happened there too. Even though I'd spent half my time drugged, I'd heard enough to give most people nightmares. But the difference between the two places was like trying to compare Chucky and Michael Myers. They were both filled with horror, but one was child's play compared to the other.

Up ahead, Boris coughed, his hand on the door. He looked over his shoulder, his soulless eyes settling on mine. The effect was akin to walking over a grave.

"You've already failed my first test. If I were you, I'd hurry. You won't like what happens if you fail me again."

His voice carried on the still night air, and all the surrounding men paused. I could feel them staring at me, waiting for me to move. My mind screamed at me to fight. To do something, anything. But I simply stood there, staring back at a monster.

For his size, Boris was amazingly fast and

light on his feet. The sight of him barreling toward me, cold fury contorting his face, would be forever etched in my mind. My body stiffened even as it shook, preparing for the blow, only to have him halt a few feet away.

We stood there for the space of a few heartbeats, just staring at one another before he finally spoke. "I'm forbidden from marring your body, but keep in mind that still leaves a lot of torture techniques for me to work with. Until you're sold, little girl, you belong to me. And it doesn't matter how much you fight, scream, or beg, you will obey. They all do in the end."

CHAPTER 12

SWITCH

What kind of *Little House On The Prairie* bullshit was Hunter trying to pull, 'cause this for damn sure wasn't a warehouse. There was nothing here but grassy fields, a stand of trees, a white picket fence, and a dirt road. Yet, according to the pin he'd dropped to my phone, I had arrived.

If that fucker double crossed me, and I ended up losing Stel, I was going to kill him. Slowly and painfully. Everyone knew I was lethal with a dart, and by the time I was done with him his balls would look like pincushions.

Without her, I had nothing. No home, no family, and no heart. I'd left it all with her when I walked out the door. If she ceased to exist, then so would I. Right after I took care of Hunter.

The rumble of a bike coming up the road behind me gave me pause. Maybe I wouldn't have to kill Hunter after all. I still had no idea why he wanted to meet in the middle of bumfuck nowhere, but whatever. As long as I got Stel back, I didn't really give a fuck either way.

A bike's headlight illuminated the still night as it rounded the last bend, and I twisted around on my seat to see who was approaching. My hand automatically reached for the pistol I had tucked into the shoulder holster underneath my vest. It wouldn't be wise to assume just because there was a biker approaching the place Hunter sent me to that they were a Devil.

In the dark, all I could only make out was the outline of two riders. Shit. All the Devil's I knew rode alone. My hand tightened around the grip of my pistol, and I hoped this was nothing more than a couple out for a late-night ride through the countryside.

The bike slowed, and as it drew closer, the riders appeared to float above the road. There was only one person I knew with a custom paint job like that.

Ryder had a Stella special, though not intentionally. His bitchy flame of the moment had pissed her off, so she painted pink flames on the side of his gas tank. He tried to order more of the manufacturer's basic black to cover it up, but suddenly nobody within a hundred-mile radius had it in stock. Then, the idiot thought he'd be slick and order it from a guy four counties over. Only, when he opened the can of paint, it was pink instead of black.

Could I have saved him a lot of time and trouble by telling him Stel knew most of the paint guys in Texas? Yeah. But where was the fun in that? Besides, it forced him to apologize for not having Stel's back, which he should have, and he ended up with something way better than a manufacturer's basic black paint job.

Honestly, I didn't know how Stel got her hands on some *Vantablack* paint considering it wasn't available commercially, but I thought it best not to go down that rabbit hole. *Vantablack* had a lot of scientific applications, but in its paint form it erased all the contours from an image, making a three-dimensional object appear two-dimensional. Thus, Ryder's bike was damn near invisible after dark.

He pulled up beside me and nodded his head at the hand I still had wrapped around my pistol. "Save that shit for when we have company later. You remember Val, don't you?"

My eyes swung to his passenger. Valentina Castillo. The only daughter of Miguel Castillo, the largest drug lord in Mexico. Or at least he was until Valentina's older brother Diego killed him and took over. Not that I was complaining about the change in management. Diego was a hell of a lot more stable than his father.

"Yeah."

Valentina's shadow shifted, and I could feel her eyes on me, sizing me up. I wasn't sure what she was hoping to find in the dark, but as far as I was concerned, she could fuck right off with her holier than thou attitude. Not that long ago, she'd been the one who was a threat. Hell, for all I knew she still was. But that was Ryder's problem, not mine.

"So, what's the plan?" I asked, swinging my gaze back to Ryder.

"Hunter wanted to meet at his place because Brandy's got something for us. Come on. We're late."

He didn't wait for my reply, not that I had one since I was still stuck on Hunter having his own place. Though I wasn't sure why that surprised me. Hunter had always guarded his privacy the way Scrooge guarded his gold. Down a dirt road, in the middle of nowhere, was actually quite fitting. You could hide a lot of bodies out here.

Whoever the hell this Brandy chick was, I hoped for her sake she could handle Hunter, or I feared she'd wind up being buried along with the rest of Hunter's problems. Hell, if I didn't get my head out of my ass, I might be joining her.

Ryder's headlights reflected off a group of

bikes parked in the grass beside a van that belonged to the club. To my left they'd strung twinkle lights all along the banister of the wraparound porch.

What the fuck was this shit? I'd been dropped into an alternate dimension where Hunter had somehow been domesticated. Wonder if he still had both his balls or if they'd been strung up on the porch too.

Ahead of me, Valentina picked her way along the lit flagstone path in her high heels. Jesus Christ. Did that girl even own a pair of tennis shoes? If not, I wondered what she wore when she worked out. An image of her prissy ass, nose stuck up in the air, running in heels on a treadmill popped into my head.

Thankfully, my snort was drowned out by the front door swinging open. Valentina walked inside like she owned the joint and I followed suit.

If Hunter wanted you dead, you'd be dead, though I doubted he'd kill her for not knocking first. He might doll out plenty of death sentences, but unlike his father, he didn't enjoy killing any more than the rest of us did.

I didn't know shit about interior design, but even I could see this place was gorgeous yet simple. A wooden bench with fancy hooks lined the left side of the entry, Valentina's heels clicking against the light wood floors. At the end of a short, dimly lit hallway, the space opened up.

Some brothers leaned against the back of a giant gray sectional, while the rest sat around the long, rectangular wooden table beside it. Hunter stood off to the side in a spacious white and black kitchen, his eyes focused on the table.

How he could stare, unblinking like that, had always creeped me the fuck out. God help whoever he was fixated on. Still, I was kinda curious because it was unusual for him to give a shit about another human being.

Then I turned my head and saw her. Talk about trippy. It was Cherry, but not. At least I didn't think it was. Not unless Cherry could magically grow her hair, and if she could, I doubted she'd be hanging out with us.

There was something else, too, but I wasn't sure what to call it. Fuck. Maybe an aura? Where Cherry gave off sunny, bubbly vibes, this girl was...walled off. Almost somber.

Ryder's shoulder brushed against mine, but instead of walking past, he stood beside me, his eyes coming to rest on the girl. "That's Brandy. She's Cherry's twin and Hunter's old lady."

"Shit," I muttered, glancing around to see if anyone had heard my slip.

Ryder, that asshole, had the nerve to snort, drawing more than one set of eyes.

"Did I mention that she's also Stella's BFF?" He leaned in and whispered, "Better get used to spending a lot of quality time with Hunter," before patting me on the back and walking away.

Like hell I would. Being forced to rely on Hunter's help for Stel's sake was one thing, but us being Friday night double date buddies wasn't happening. Anyone who lacked the ability to feel wasn't all the way right in the head, and while that trait came in handy for cleaning up the club's messes, it didn't exactly make him comfortable to be around.

Ryder clapped his hands, drawing everyone's attention. "Listen up! Brandy has been working tirelessly behind the scenes to help us find Stella and thinks she found something that may help us."

He nodded his head at Brandy, whose cheeks were getting pinker by the minute. Interesting. If she was this flustered around the guys, I wondered how in the hell she handled Stel. I loved the girl to death, but she was about as subtle as a bull in a China shop and cursed like a sailor.

She shifted in her seat as she fingered the pearls around her neck, but when she spoke, her voice was confident and clear. "Her abductors have deviated from their usual pattern. Once the bidding starts, they normally won't post again until the clock runs out and they announce the winner. Then the name is left on the site for twenty-four hours before all traces of the auction are removed."

"About an hour ago"—she turned her laptop

around—"this photo was added. I've magnified and enhanced the background so you can get a feel for the layout of the room. While it's not as valuable as a blueprint, I figured it was better than you guys going in blind."

Moving closer, I tried to brace myself for whatever image might be on her screen. It couldn't be any worse than the shit I had rolling through my head right now. But imagining shit and having it stare you in the face were two very different things.

As I gazed at the photo, I released the breath I'd been holding.

"I don't see Stella," Tweak said, his arm brushing against hers as he leaned closer. "How do you know if it's really her or one of the other girls?"

Brandy shrank back as if he'd burned her by moving a fraction of an inch. A low growl came from the direction of the kitchen and Tweak leaned back in his chair, rolling his eyes at Hunter.

"Calm your ass down over there. Everyone knows you've already licked this cookie, and I barely bumped the lid on the jar." He crossed his arms and nodded at Brandy. "How do you live with that psycho?"

She let out a half giggle, half snort, her cheeks going from pink to red. "Subtle, Tweak, very subtle."

My eyes wandered around the room as I

tried to figure out what I was missing because obviously something was up with this girl. Unfortunately, the guys remained silent and unfazed, waiting on her to continue. Hell, maybe I was imagining things. It had been months since my head had been this clear.

"She wasn't in the picture"—she let out a shaky breath—"because I edited her out. I knew she wouldn't have wanted any of you to see her like that." She looked down at the table, her voice a choked whisper when she spoke again. "It's not as if it would have helped you find her any faster."

The room grew silent, all the men uncomfortably shifting in their spots. Well, almost all of them.

One minute Hunter was standing in the kitchen, and the next he was beside her. He'd always been able to move like a whisper of wind. Normally, it creeped me out because it reminded me of how dangerous he was. But not today.

As I watched him scoop her up and cart her off down a hallway, I saw a different side to Hunter. The care he showed her was completely unlike him. Hunter wasn't capable of love, but clearly, he felt something akin to it for this woman.

A woman who knew Stel well enough to know that it would have killed her for the guys to see her as a victim. There was nothing Stel feared more than her own vulnerability, and it warmed my heart to know that Brandy not only understood my girl, but was looking out for her.

Gunner reached for the laptop and moved it closer, his hair fisted in his hand to keep it away from his face. "It's going to be a bitch getting all of them out safely."

The prospect that had eyed me curiously at the clubhouse raised a dark brow. "All of them? I thought we were only interested in Mad Dog's daughter."

His voice was so smooth it was almost a soft purr. There was something vaguely familiar in the way he rolled his *s*'s and *r*'s.

"When I said all, I fucking meant all," Gunner barked at him, his old army days coming out with the command and weight of his voice. "You might be okay with leaving women locked up in cages like dogs, but I am not."

"Me either," Beast spoke up, resting both elbows on the table and stroking a massive hand down his dark beard. "But how big of a bitch are we talking here? She slashed a bike tire or poked a hole in the condom?"

"Jesus, who the hell have you been fucking?"

Beast raised his giant sausage of a middle finger in Tweak's direction while his dark eyes watched Gunner.

"If they were cuffed or behind some type of chain link enclosure, we could have had them out in no time with the bolt cutters. Hopefully, before the guards even knew we were there."

Gunner sighed, his breath ruffling the ends of his hair. "But the sick bastards have converted the warehouse into a damn prison. The only way we're getting to the women is with a key, and that doubles the odds of them being used as human shields. Saw that shit enough over in the Middle East and I'd rather not relive it in my own goddamned country."

Hunter walked back into the room then, alone this time, and Ryder looked over at him. "Is she all right?"

"No, but she will be. Let's get this shit done so she won't have to worry herself sick over it anymore."

Ryder blew out a breath. "Did you get a look at the picture?"

"Of course." Hunter raised his brow, his dead eyes unsettling.

"We're going to try to get the women out before we clean house, so if you see the chance to grab the keys, do it."

Hunter nodded and Ryder looked over at Colt. "You hang back and take comm duty. Keep Hunter up to date on all outside activity, including any threats Gunner and Val have to neutralize. If Hunter should tell you things are going to shit on his end, call me."

"Roger that, Prez."

"And nobody goes in until I say so." Ryder looked directly at me as he said, "Is that understood?"

All the men mumbled their agreement except me. That was a promise I just couldn't keep.

Ryder was on me in two strides, his nose nearly touching mine. "I said, is that understood?"

He and I had never come to blows before. Not even close. But before the night was over, we just might. Nobody was going to stop me from getting Stel back. Nobody.

"I'll toe your fucking line," I said through clenched teeth. "Until I catch a whiff that something isn't right. Then I'm going in and killing everything in sight because there's nothing, and I mean nothing, more important to me than Stel."

His dark eyes bored into mine, but it was Pops's lazy drawl I heard coming from the table. "If a bullfrog had wings, he wouldn't bump his ass when he jumped."

Ryder's old man had a habit of randomly dropping southern sayings like they were weird little wisdom nuggets. Normally, I found it amusing, mostly because it seemed to get under Ryder's skin. Today, not so much. We needed to get moving rather than sit around decoding whatever the fuck it was he just said.

Ryder let out a frustrated breath, his eyes flicking over to the kitchen table before returning to mine. "Spit out whatever the hell it is you're trying to say because I don't have time for bull. Frog or otherwise."

"Damn young bloods," Mad Dog muttered as he shifted in his chair beside Pops. "He's trying to say that demanding Switch follow orders tonight is like wishing for the impossible. If it were Valentina in there, you know damn well you wouldn't be waiting around on an order. Now, I vote we get the fuck out of here and you boys can settle your shit after I get my daughter back."

Mad Dog, like his daughter, wasn't one to mince words. Right now, it was my favorite thing about him.

"I couldn't have said it better."

"Fine," Ryder bit out, his eyes narrowing to slits. "Switch, you're with me."

CHAPTER 13

STELLA

Bile climbed up my throat as Boris stood behind me, his giant hands spanning my waist, his tongue leaving a wet trail up the side of my neck. Guards stood all around us in the wide expanse between the two rows of prison cells. Even with the dim lighting, there was no mistaking the way they stroked themselves as they watched. The entire thing sickened me until I could feel it like a poison eating away at my soul.

"Manuel, I think it's time you turn her over. Our guest of honor hasn't yet had the pleasure of seeing her beautiful tear-streaked face."

The guard grunted his acknowledgment, and I shut my eyes. This situation was beyond fucked-up. How was I supposed to look her in the eye knowing I stood by and did nothing while this asshole had his way with her in front of everyone?

She would clearly see that I was naked and in chains, unable to help anyone, even myself, but that didn't mean she wouldn't still hold a grudge. Hell, if I were in her shoes I would. It might not be logical, but nothing about this situation was normal.

My chains rattled with the force of Boris's shake, his hiss against my ear jolting me from my fucked-up train of thought. "If you shut those pretty eyes of yours again, I'll tell him to use her ass next, and around here, lube is a privilege."

"No," I whispered, the high ceilings echoing my tortured words back to me.

When I opened my eyes, all I could see were the screams hidden in the depths of her dark, haunted eyes. Moisture pooled at the corners, but her tears refused to fall, the sight gutting me surer than any knife.

Her skin was pale, like that of a China doll, which only made the dark smudges beneath her eyes even more noticeable. But it was her face that robbed me of breath. The sharp cut of her jawline, the slightly sunken cheeks with the deep dimple, and the almost oblong shape of her face were unmistakable. She was the thing Jules had been willing to die for.

This girl, however inadvertently, had placed me at the gates of hell. Yet, I couldn't summon up a shred of animosity toward her. How could I when she was right here with me, her sentence far longer and more brutal than mine?

Which begged the question, if a strong, capable man like Jules could have his family taken, then were any of us safe? Suddenly it wasn't her face I saw, it was Cherry's. All the light gone from her hazel eyes the way they'd been leached from this girl's eyes, and I couldn't bear it.

The nail I'd been holding on to slipped from my hand and fell to the floor with a barely recognized tinkle. There was no way I could use it now. Not knowing these soulless men would just take another in my place.

Heavy boot falls announced the arrival of another guard. Jesus, how many of these sick fuckers were going to come around the corner and whip their dicks out?

This guy didn't stop though, instead opting to go the long way around the set of metal benches at the center of the room. When he finally reached us, he didn't spare a glance for the girl splayed over the bench in front of us. Nor did he seem to notice me, standing in front of Boris, naked as the day I was born.

"I'm sorry to disturb you, boss"—his eyes flicked to mine and then back to Boris's—"but you know who asked me to give you a message."

He pulled a small yellow slip of paper from the pocket of his black fatigues and handed it over. Boris waved him off with a flick of his hand, and he quickly left the same way he'd come from.

Behind me, I could hear paper rustling, and I chanced a peek over my shoulder. Boris held the note up, the backside of it disappointingly blank, while he read. When he was done, he crumpled up the paper and shoved it into his pocket.

His smile was positively feral as he gazed down at me from his towering height. "It seems you're due for a photo op."

A shiver slid down my spine as he looked over the top of my head at someone behind me. "Manuel, when you're finished with her, put her back in her cell. Today's demonstration is at an end."

Boris then dragged me by the arm, his fingers digging painfully into my flesh, over to the bench at the center of the room. My lungs seized up as I contemplated what sort of plans he had in store for me.

Was this some kind of bizarre buy a girl against her will pinup, or was the purpose of taking my picture purely to antagonize the club? Honestly, with these assholes, it could go either way.

CHAPTER 14

STELLA

The passage of time was no longer marked by the ticking of a clock, but by the sound of approaching boots. Each shift rotated positions at regular intervals, but so far nobody new had entered the mix. After about the fifth rotation, I'd learned to distinguish between the different footfalls of the guards.

The only real guarantee of safety came with silence, but when I heard a sure, quick, flatfooted approach, I wasn't overly concerned. Outside of double checking the cell doors and bringing us bread or water, the messenger guard from before never paid us any mind. I never thought I'd be thankful to be treated as a bothersome chore.

My cell here was like the last one, only far newer. The sink didn't drip, the mattress didn't have any stains, and I could pee without wanting to get a tetanus shot afterward. This place was also considerably larger, with enough cells to house thirty girls even though only about twenty of them were currently occupied.

They hadn't brought in any more girls after me, but a few were led away in chains, their cells remaining empty. Whether they'd been sold, or were just being moved like I was, I didn't know. Guards around here had loose lips whenever they thought we were all asleep, but they mainly talked about upcoming assignments and the pussy at each facility like the fucking assholes they were.

But, hey at least Boris hadn't graced me with his presence since our impromptu photo shoot. If you could call it that. He'd strung me up and stepped on my bare foot with the heel of his boot while another guard snapped the pic. Then they'd thrown me in a cell and left me alone. Which was fine by me. I was in no rush to return to Boris's side and play any more of his sick games.

As it was, every time I shut my eyes, I saw her face. The girl Jules had risked everything for. All the pent-up anger and resentment I'd once felt for him was gone. I should be relieved, but all it made me feel was empty.

Maybe Boris had succeeded in breaking me. Lots of people had tried and failed over the years, but for him it had been child's play. He'd been right about one thing. The man was an expert at torture, and he didn't even have to touch a hair on your head to do it.

Heavy footfalls echoed outside my cell like the march of an executioner. He'd finally come back for me. My fight-or-flight instincts had let me down thus far, but at some point, my sense of self-preservation had to kick in. Didn't it?

Boris filled the space on the other side of the bars, and I felt myself shrinking back. His demented grin only made his ugly face seem even more wrong as he unlocked the bars and slid them aside.

"Are you coming out, or should I go in after you?"

My legs shook, and I wasn't even sure how I was able to stand, but I wasn't about to be stuck in a small space with this monster. It was wobbly at best, but I lifted my head and concentrated on a speck of lint clinging to his shoulder. Stupidly, it helped. The monster of my nightmares had morphed back into a man. A beast of man, but a man nonetheless.

He moved to the right of the door to let me pass, his bushy brows drawn down into what could possibly be a frown. Then again, it could also be disappointment. Either way, he didn't waste any time grabbing my arm in his punishing grip and dragging me along the row of benches. My heart fluttered wildly in my chest, waiting for him to stop at one, but he kept going.

A guard stood on either side of an open doorway, both of them nodding to Boris as he shoved me inside and closed the door. This room was something straight out of a horror film, and I backed right into his chest and froze. His hand clamped down around my wrist and it was as if someone had flipped my switch.

My nails clawed at any piece of available skin I could reach as the heel of my foot came down on the top of his boot. Pain shot up my leg and his laughter made me fight even harder. I kicked, bucked, swatted, and clawed for all I was worth, but no matter what I did, we kept getting closer to the hospital bed at the center of the room.

Fuck this and fuck him.

He howled when I bit down on his forearm, but kept moving toward the abomination at the center of the room. My legs dangled as he finally lifted me, my fists pounding against his head and back as he shackled one of my legs. The other caught him in the side of the face, for all the good it did me, before he shackled that one.

Blood ran down his face and his nose looked a little crooked by the time he attached my hands to either side of the bed.

We looked at each other, both of our chests

heaving, me naked and splayed while he seemed totally unaffected. He didn't even bother wiping off the blood seeping from his nose, instead opting to move closer and let it drip onto my thigh.

"Someone's eager to play."

"Fuck you," I hissed, frantically pulling on my arms.

The leather manacles cut into my wrists, but I didn't care. I'd gotten a glimpse of all the shit laid out on the table beside me and attached to the walls. Toys that mingled pleasure with pain, only I didn't need to be told there was only going to be pain.

"That's certainly on the table"—he chuckled —"but I'll need to prepare you first."

My body thrashed like a fish out of water. He could fuck right off if he thought I was going to make this easy for him. Not that it fazed him any. He took his time arranging the torture devices spread out on the table.

The corner of his lips curled upward as he climbed on top of me. His massive legs pinned my arms down, his fly eye level with my face. Let that fucker whip his dick out. I'd bite that shit clean off.

"Tsk, tsk," he hummed as he leaned back and grabbed something I couldn't see off the table.

I felt a pinch on my clit like he'd clamped something onto it, which was uncomfortable as hell, but didn't hurt. At least, not until he gave it a good yank.

A tortured scream broke free from my lips, black dots dancing before my eyes.

"Beautiful," I heard him mutter before he pulled on whatever it was again.

Everything in the room dimmed, the blinding lights above me fading into the shadows. The dark edges swirled and twisted like mist until they revealed a pair of cinnamon eyes. They darkened to almost a whiskey color as they roamed over my face before he slowly leaned in until all I could see were the blacks of his pupils.

His breath was a mixture of spearmint and menthol as it ghosted across my face, and I closed my eyes as he moved his head to the side and buried his nose in my neck. The hair from his beard tickled my jaw as he inhaled. His breath was deliciously hot against my neck, and I shivered as he inhaled again, deeper this time, like I was his air.

He lifted his head, and I opened my eyes, wanting to study every detail. It had been so long since I'd seen his face. Too long.

His brows drew together, and he opened his mouth, but nothing came out. He tried again and again, growing more frantic each time he tried.

Suddenly, blinding pain bit into my jaw like a million fire ants had all bit me at once, and then he was gone. Bright lights exploded behind my eyes and when I blinked, I was right back in hell with the devil's face above mine.

"I'll not allow you to escape, even if it's only into the dark recesses of your mind," he hissed as he leaned back to unzip his pants. "Let's not have a repeat of that little stunt going forward, shall we? If the bruising on your jaw doesn't fade before you're sold, I'll have to come out of pocket for the damages."

He tilted his head to the side and regarded me as he stroked himself. "Then again, crushing you under my boot might make up for it."

My jaw felt like it had its own pulse and my head pounded under the harsh glare of the lights. The room swam before my eyes and suddenly I was seeing two monsters above me instead of one.

My stomach revolted, its meager contents threatening to make a comeback. There was movement from above me, but it was like looking through a kaleidoscope, a mass of blurry shapes and colors.

"No!"

The scream that tore up my throat and echoed around the room was as foreign as his invasion. It felt as if he were trying to tear me apart from the inside out. My body involuntarily jerked against my bonds, and I screwed my eyes tightly shut to block out the horror of what was happening.

But that was next to impossible. There was no way to escape the sound of his sadistic grunts as he stole something from me that I knew I'd never get back. My peace of mind.

Fat wet drops peppered my face, and I licked my lips tentatively, a decidedly metallic taste filling my mouth. Boris's weight went from skin crawling to crushing in an instant and my eyes shot open.

There Hunter stood, looking like a blood-soaked avenging angel. I couldn't believe my eyes and blinked a few times, but his image never wavered.

He didn't say a word as he shoved Boris off me, his body landing on the floor with a thud. Hunter's light blue eyes roamed over my body in that clinically detached way of his as he cut my bindings, Boris's blood still dripping from his knife. When he was done, he held out his bloody hand.

"Can you walk?"

Could I walk? That was it. No trace of horror, remorse, or pity.

I'd never thought of Hunter's lack of feeling as an asset, quite the opposite actually considering my best friend had fucked up and fallen in love with him. His affliction, as he called it, made it impossible for him to look at me any differently than he had before. He was here for Brandy and the club, not me, and I was grateful for that fact.

"I think so."

I looked down at the blood coating my torso

and running down my legs. There was a metal clamp still attached to my clit, and with a detachment that I knew couldn't be normal, I removed it and threw it on top of Boris's dead body.

"Here." A plain white T-shirt landed in my lap and a broken chuckle left my parted lips. Modesty was the least of my concerns, but I put the shirt on, anyway.

"Come on. I've got to get you out of here before the cavalry arrives."

The cavalry, a.k.a. the club, were the last people I wanted to see right now. It was an ungrateful thought, considering they were springing me from hell, but I couldn't stand for them to see me like this. Bloody, detached, broken. A soulless being who only cared about one thing now.

"I didn't even get to kill him," I muttered to myself as I hopped off the bed, the room spinning on its axis.

Hunter kept me from face planting, which pissed me the fuck off. My stomach did another flip as he held me steady with one hand while I got my bearings. Shame filled me at having let these men turn me into a weak, pitiful, frail creature.

"Here." He pressed a small knife that looked more suitable for fileting fish than killing a man into my hand. "Even in your condition you should be able to finish the two guards I left immobilized at the door. As for the rest, I'm afraid I've already promised them to Switch."

My breath hitched, and a lump formed in my throat at the mere mention of his name. No! He couldn't be here. He couldn't see me. Not right now. Not like this.

"Just don't let any of them see me," I whispered to Hunter, almost falling as I tried to take a step.

He gave me a curt nod before lifting me into his arms. It was humiliating, but I'd rather this than chance running into any of the guys. Yes, that made me a coward, but as I'd recently discovered, I wasn't the badass bitch I thought I was.

Hunter stepped over two bodies slumped outside the door and stopped, gently setting me back on my feet.

"Go ahead." He nodded at the knife still clutched in my hand. "You've got five seconds to do whatever you want to them."

Hunter had just become my new best friend. Sorry, Brandy. You're a bad bitch in your own right, but he was giving me something she never could. Sweet, sweet revenge.

The room spun as I kneeled down, but I didn't care. It was worth it to see two sets of eyes watching the knife I held in horror. It was time for payback, especially considering one of them was the man who'd raped the girl Jules had died to protect.

I'd never been a violent person, but boy did it feel good to slash the throat of the asshole I didn't give two shits about. The spray of his blood across Hunter's white shirt was a badge of honor I'd proudly wear out of this shithole for every woman he'd ever terrorized.

Now, the other asshole, he wouldn't be lucky enough to receive a quick death from me. Since I was short on time, and the room refused to stay put, I was going to need Hunter's help with this one.

"Pull down his pants for me so I can cut his dick off."

The man's whimpers were like music to my ears. Honestly, I expected Hunter to balk at my request, or tell me we didn't have time for this shit. Instead, he bent over, and with quick, precise movements, did as I'd asked.

I wasn't sure what sort of gift you got someone who'd helped you make a man a eunuch, but he was getting something from me after this.

"I hope your shriveled dick follows you into hell."

The room tilted, and I fell over, his dick still in my hand. He let out a gurgled scream, then blacked out.

I threw my head back and laughed like one of those deranged evil villains off the Saturday morning cartoons. Two Hunters appeared before my eyes, both of them shaking their heads at me as if I were an errant child before lifting me into his arms.

He walked as if I were as light as a feather, cells passing us by with dizzying speed.

"Wait." My stomach rolled as he came to a halt. "There's a girl, dark hair, dark eyes, tall, arrestingly beautiful. You can't miss her. We can't leave without her."

He shook his head and kept going. "Setting the rest of the girls free is Gunner's problem, not mine. I promised to bring you straight home to Brandy, and that's exactly what I'm going to do."

I could live with that for now. Besides, what other choice did I have? The club would set the women free, Hunter said so. But I still needed to talk to one of them. Face to face.

"Fine, but I need you to ask Gunner to find that girl and bring her to me."

He didn't bat an eyelash at my request, and I was starting to see why Brandy could fall for a man like Hunter. He might not be capable of love in the conventional sense of the word, but he more than made up for it in other ways.

CHAPTER 15

SWITCH

Stel looked so fragile and broken in nothing but a T-shirt that was more red than white, her slender arms clinging to Hunter for dear life, her blond head buried in his chest. Before Ryder could stop me, I left the darkened cover of the tree line and sprinted straight for them.

Hunter slipped back through the hole in the fence that we'd cut out earlier, and kept going, his stride only breaking long enough to toss something at me. Out of instinct, I slowed to catch it, watching as he veered off toward where we'd left the bikes. My brain took a few seconds to register what I held in my hand. A set of keys.

We hadn't planned on the outside of the warehouse being lit up like the fucking Fourth of July, and when I looked up, there were already two guards closing in on the fence. Hunter had done his part, and now that Stel was safe, it was time for me to do mine.

Red clouded my vision as I slipped through the hole in the fence and pulled my gun from its holster. But before I could take aim, the men were falling to the pavement. More guards came from the direction of the warehouse as I ran, their guns raised, heedless of their comrades lying face down. Thanks to Gunner, they soon fell, one by one, like human dominos.

Unscathed, I shot the snarling dogs as they lunged and slipped through the plain black door. I traded my gun for the knife I kept strapped to my ankle because fuck shooting these bastards. None of them deserved the quick death eating a bullet would bring, and while I couldn't do anything about the ones Gunner had taken care of outside, these men were mine. They'd fucked with Stel, and before this night was over, I would feed off their terror before watching the light fade from their eyes.

Like a wraith, I moved down the darkened corridor. With every life I took, with every gasp or gurgle, I felt no remorse. If I should meet them again in hell, I'd make their death even slower and more painful.

When I reached the end, I peeked around the opening. Five guards prowled between the two rows of prison style cells, just like in the photo Brandy had shown us, their fingers resting against the triggers of the machine guns they carried.

The girl in the cell across from me whimpered, and I held my finger against my lips, shaking my head. She trembled as she flattened herself against the wall but remained quiet.

Slipping my knife into the side pocket of my cargo pants for easy access, I withdrew my gun from its holster and fired five shots in quick succession. Each shot hit its intended target, but I fired a second round to make sure the men stayed down.

Contrary to popular belief, Ryder hadn't chosen me to be his VP merely because we were childhood friends. Only those closest to me knew that shooting a gun came as naturally to me as throwing a dart. Maybe it was because they both required a certain focus and dexterity that quieted my demons. Whatever the reason, it had always seemed unwise to advertise what I was capable of.

These fuckers had just gotten a front-row seat to my little hidden talent, but based on their wide-eyed stares, I'd say they hardly appreciated my demonstration. One of them attempted to spit on my boots but thought better of it when I threatened to cut out his tongue before I slit his throat.

By the time the rest of the guys stormed into the room a few minutes later, weapons drawn, blood dripped from my fingers and there was only one man still left alive. He tried to use his good leg to crawl away, but Ryder put a stop to his progress with a bullet to the back of his head.

"You good?" he asked, looking over at me.

I wiped the blade of my knife against my thigh, the black of my pants hiding the red stain. "Yeah."

"Jesus, man," Tweak said, stepping over a stream of blood on his way to where Beast stood next to another open doorway. At his feet lay two bodies I hadn't had the pleasure of killing. "It looks like Jeffrey Dahmer hit up a rave in here."

"Good one, dude," Beast said, frowning down at the floor. "Tweak, am I imagining things or is that a dick lying next to that guy?"

Tweak had a look, his normally tan complexion taking on a decidedly green hue. He covered his junk and looked over at me in horror.

I shrugged. "Wasn't me."

Tweak looked back over at Beast. "Hunter?"

"Nah," he said, his lower lip curling as his dark eyes met mine. "I think he made the mistake of fucking with the wrong woman."

Stel hated to appear weak in front of anyone, especially a man, so if Hunter had to carry her out of here, it was because she couldn't walk on her own. Yet, the girl had still castrated a man.

Pride swelled in my chest, knowing that my girl had given them hell until the very end.

Colt looked up from his phone, his brows drawing together. "Hunter's tried texting Gunner, but he hasn't responded yet."

"Ask him what's up," Ryder said as he walked over to where Colt stood in the center of the room. "I'm sure Gunner just hasn't checked his phone. Him and Val are dismantling the long-range rifles while they wait for Pops and Dagger to pick them up in the van."

Colt's phone dinged, and he held it up so Ryder could read the message on his screen. Both of them looked over to the doorway where Beast and Tweak still stood.

Ryder cocked his brow. "Stella wants us to bring her back the dark-haired girl and insists Tweak will know which one she's talking about when he sees her."

"Don't look at me like that. I doubt any of the girls I've ever fucked are locked up here."

"You never know," Beast said with a shrug. "The odds are pretty good. You've fucked a lot of chicks."

"Shit," he grumbled as he trudged over to the row of cells behind me. "You're right. I better have a look."

A few of the girls sniffed or shifted, but none of them said anything to him as he passed. When he got to the far end, he shook his head and started down the other side. He hadn't gone very far when he halted, his eyes glued to whoever was in that cell.

"Who is it?"

Ryder had just asked the million-dollar question. Stel was akin to a coconut, you had to get past her tough outer layers before you got to the sweet goodness that lay underneath. So, color me suspicious, but I had a lot of questions for this girl, whoever she was. Starting with how she and Stel had become that close while locked in separate cages.

"I'll know for sure in a second." Tweak cocked his head to the side and asked, "Sweetheart, by any chance do you have a brother named Jules?"

That name wasn't ringing any bells, so I snuck a sideways glance at Ryder. Judging by the pursing of his lips, he didn't have a clue about what was going on, either.

"Yes," she said, her voice cracking as if it hadn't been used in very a long time. She cleared her throat and tried again, a set of long, pale fingers winding around the bars. "Did he send you?"

"No, but we've been looking for him. Seems he vanished around the same time as my friend." His voice took on a hard edge as he asked, "Would you happen to know anything about that?"

Stepping over the body at my feet, I stomped over to her cell, staring into it, my face a scant few inches away from hers. If this girl knew who took Stel, I wanted names, and I wanted them now. It would be up to her whether she willingly gave them to me. While I'd never hurt a woman before, I was willing to make an exception. Fuck an eye for an eye. I wanted an eye for a soul.

"No." Her dark soulless eyes held mine captive like a monster who'd sank their claws deep into my throat. "But my brother couldn't have had anything to do with her disappearance."

"What makes you so sure," I gritted out, my hands on either side of hers tightening around the bars.

She backed away, her hands falling to her sides as she said, "Because he's in the CIA."

CHAPTER 16

STELLA

I sat on the shower floor, my chin resting on my knees, watching as a river of red snaked its way toward the drain. Steam enveloped me in a protective cocoon, yet I hardly felt safe. Logically, I knew he was never coming back, Hunter had made sure of that by slitting his throat, yet I couldn't seem to help it. Every time I closed my eyes, all I saw was his face.

Not even a vat of holy water, if I believed in that sort of thing, could cleanse me of his touch. It was like a piece of him had crawled beneath my skin and latched on.

Goose bumps raised the hair on my arms despite the hot water pelting my skin. The sting of it should have served as a reminder that I'd survived. Only, it didn't feel like I had. Not all of me, at least.

The bathroom door swung open, cloud puffs escaping through the gap, before it closed again. My heart thudded against my ribcage, and I buried my head, curling in on myself. No, not here. Not again. Not right now.

A second later, the faint scent of roses reached my nostrils, and I peeked over the top of my knees.

Brandy opened the glass shower door just enough to squeeze through, the water instantly soaking her white button-up shirt and chinos. She sat down across from me, her blond hair hanging limply in her face as she mimicked my pose.

Neither one of us said anything, but it wasn't an uncomfortable sort of silence that you felt compelled to fill. She just sat there, blinking away the water as it dripped from her lashes.

If I screamed or told her to fuck off right now, she probably wouldn't even bat an eyelash. She'd let me unleash the well of pent-up emotions churning in my gut, poisoning me from the inside out, because she understood what few people ever could.

She never talked about it, but I'd put enough pieces together to know that we now belonged to the same fucked-up club. Maybe we should get buttons, jackets, or something made that said man-haters. Then again, ball busters had a nice ring to it.

Only, unlike Brandy, whose fear had never left her, mine was rapidly dissolving into something much more destructive.

"Fuck!"

It had always been my favorite curse word because of its versatility. Some people thought if you used vulgar language that you were ignorant or didn't have a big vocabulary. Not true. There were plenty of words I could have used, but the wretched and unholy state of things just didn't resonate the same as fuck. 'Cause that's what we were. Fucked.

"How do you keep from seeing him every time you close your eyes?"

All I wanted to do was forget about what happened, forget about him, but how could I do that with his image burned into my retinas.

"Find yourself a more frightening monster."

There it was. The thing that drew her to Hunter. I finally understood why he was different. She'd found a monster willing to kill hers. Literally. But I didn't hold out any hope that things would be that simple for me. Her monster had killed mine, and it hadn't done a damn thing for me.

The bathroom door cracked open, Hunter's monotone voice coming from the other side.

"Stella, the guys brought back that dark-haired girl for you."

Facing my father, and the club, was more than I could handle right now. It was going to take everything I had just to stand, say nothing about waltzing down the hall and telling a woman who'd just escaped from hell that her loved one was dead because of me.

"She's the only one I want to see. Please ask my dad and the guys to give me some space right now."

There was a long pause, and if there wasn't still steam escaping through the bathroom door, I'd have thought he left.

"I'm afraid I can't do that. Until Ryder's had the chance to question her, she's not to be left alone."

Hunter wasn't making any sense. Her only tie to the club was through me, and based on the grime plastered to her skin I'd say she was taken some time ago. There was no way she could have known Antonio sent Jules to watch me, let alone what he'd done for her. Which was something I'd take with me to the grave. She'd suffered enough without carrying around that little guilt nugget.

"What does Ryder want with her?"

"He thinks she's the best shot we have at finding your missing CIA agent boyfriend."

What the fuck? He had to have been talking about Jules because nobody knew I was still technically with Antonio. Still, it was a shock.

Jules had been Antonio's most trusted right-hand man, and I found it odd with how paranoid Antonio was that in five years' time he'd never once fingered Jules for an agent. Not that any of it mattered now. Jules was no longer a threat to any of us.

"Hunter, you can let her go. She won't be able to help you because Jules isn't missing."

My muscles protested when I uncurled my limbs to stand. Brandy immediately shot to her feet to help me, but I shook my head. It took me a few tries, and I was dizzy as hell, but I finally stood on my own two feet.

"He's dead."

CHAPTER 17

SWITCH

"What are you doing out here? I thought you told Ryder you were going back to the hotel to get some sleep."

When I looked over my shoulder, a tiny orange dot burned brightly from the shadows beneath the old oak tree.

"Yeah, and I thought you quit smoking. Again."

Mad Dog had fallen into and out of love with nicotine more times than any person I'd ever met. When his wife was alive, it was a game the two of them played. He'd try his best to hide it, Pat would confront him about his "cancer sticks," he'd quit, and after a while the cycle would repeat.

When she died, I thought for sure he'd quit swinging back and forth on his cigarette pendulum. Then, a few weeks later, Stel stormed into the bar, pulled the cigarette from between his lips, and put it out in his beer. He'd looked over at me, winked, pulled out a stick of gum, and popped it into his mouth. I guess they both needed to pretend that things were normal in order to heal and move on.

"Nah, Stel just hasn't caught me yet." The orange dot bobbed in the darkness as he walked toward me. "But don't you worry, she will."

So, that was his angle. He was hoping to goad Stel into talking to him. Yeah, good luck with that one old man. Stel was hiding behind her watchdog, Brandy, and hadn't spoken to anyone in the club in the past thirty-six hours.

Hunter was the one who told us that Stel refused to see anyone from the club and what had happened to the missing CIA agent. Ryder told the rest of the guys to give her some space but wisely kept his mouth shut when it came to me. He'd been back to check on her every day, but her answer was always the same.

"Might want to try smoking in front of the window, then," I said with a shake of my head.

"Can't be too obvious about it, or she'll know what I'm up to."

He stopped beside me, the twinkle lights on the porch casting shadows over his face as he blew smoke out of the corner of his mouth. "What do you make of the dark-haired girl being holed up in there with them? Something ain't right, but I can't put my finger on it."

"I don't like it either, but I trust Stel. If she says the girl doesn't know anything then she doesn't know anything."

"Normally I'd agree, but with what she just went through..." He put the cigarette to his lips, his hand shaking slightly as he inhaled, then blew out a breath. "She ain't exactly thinking clearly right now."

I looked up at the large front window of Hunter's place, hoping Stel would walk past. These days, that was the only way I could see her, with a pane of glass separating us. Once in a while I'd catch her standing there, staring out the front window, but then she'd see me, and back away.

With a lit cigarette between his lips, he pulled out the pack he kept hidden in the inside pocket of his cut and handed me one. When he patted his jeans pocket, I shook my head, and pulled out the silver lighter with The Deviants logo in the center that Stel had gotten me a few years back.

"That's why I've asked Hunter to keep a close eye on the girl. I can't imagine a human trafficking ring as sophisticated as this one not doing their homework first, and taking the sister of a CIA agent is the type of fuckup that would bring the entire operation down."

Unlike Mad Dog, my love affair with nicotine began when I was fifteen and discovered that it helped me to focus, and I'd never once thought of quitting. There was something about that first hit to my system that calmed the mass of competing thoughts inside my head so I could organize them. Unfortunately, I didn't like where those thoughts were leading.

"You ever consider that whoever is behind this might be using the club as a smoke screen?"

He rubbed a hand along his jaw. "What are you thinking?"

Don't get me wrong, the club had plenty of enemies, and I wasn't ruling any of them out, but too many things just weren't adding up for me. Mad Dog wasn't wrong. Something was off.

"If this was club related, then why not go after either the president's or vice president's old ladies? And why take Stel's"—it physically pained me to say this—"boyfriend? It would have been easier for them to either wait for her to be alone or kill him when he went to take a piss. Once they had Stel, what did they need him for? You and I both know that anyone can be made to talk under the right set of circumstances."

As I inhaled more of that sweet nicotine into my lungs, one thought kept circling like a buzzard over its kill, waiting for the right time to strike. No doubt this had already occurred to Hunter, because the man was always ten steps ahead of everyone, but it wouldn't hurt to state my intentions.

Since I'd gone nomad, I didn't really need this charter's permission to do shit, but that didn't mean I had a desire to go stepping on anyone's toes. When walking around Hunter's backyard, especially, you should be damn clear about why you were there unless you wanted to wind up in an early grave.

"There's only one reason Hunter would have received an invitation to that auction. Someone out there wanted us to find her, and once Stel is well enough, I intend to find out who that someone is. No one does favors for free, and I'd rather not be blindsided by the return request. If you catch my drift."

"I do, but do you think it's wise to involve Stella?"

"Don't kid yourself, old man." I patted his back and shook my head. He didn't know his daughter very well if he thought for one second that she was going to sit this one out. "Stel will be out for blood, and I intend to be right there beside her as she bathes in it."

CHAPTER 18

STELLA

After I broke the news of Jules's death, the girl sat there, staring at a point over my shoulder. Her utter stillness and lack of a reaction were a little disturbing, and frankly creeped me the fuck out, but I tried not to judge her. Everyone dealt with grief in their own way and the girl had already been through hell before this piece of unwelcome news.

My eyes darted over to where Brandy sat, her mouth pulled down at the corners, and her blond brow furrowed as she stared at her. Well, shit. She was supposed to be helping me out here. Brandy might be a little socially awkward, but let's call a spade a spade, I was a bull moose on the best of days.

I cleared my throat, and Brandy jerked in her seat, her hazel eyes meeting mine. My brows rose, and I hoped to fuck she'd take the hint because now that I'd said what I needed to, I was dangerously close to face planting into her couch cushions.

"Well, ah…" Brandy floundered for a moment before finally saying, "I'm sorry, nobody ever told me your name."

My sleep addled brain wondered if I'd even thought to ask what it was before I just blurted out that Jules was dead because of me. Fuck. Me and my big mouth strike again.

"Delilah," she supplied woodenly.

At least she was talking, which was a good sign. Right? Maybe she'd just gone into shock or some shit and that was why she was…zombie-ish. Which, at this point, I wasn't even sure was a thing. I rubbed at my eyes, hard, and blinked, my vision slightly fuzzy.

"Delilah," Brandy repeated, testing out her name. "Can we get you a cup of tea? Maybe call someone for you?"

"No." She slowly turned her head toward Brandy, and a shiver went down my spine because it was some shit straight out of a horror movie. "There is no one to call." She blinked rapidly and then suddenly shouted, "They killed the only person I had left!"

Her whole body vibrated with the force of her words, her hands balled into tight fists in her lap, and her chest heaved. This was an emotion I understood, an emotion I could get behind, and one that fed mine like a shot of adrenaline to the veins.

I leaned forward, sucking air through my teeth, too tired to hide the pain that racked my battered body. "Then what do you say we take those fuckers down? First, we take their money, and then we take their lives."

The room spun, and darkness crowded the edges of my vision. Exhaustion pulled at me, and my elbow slipped off my leg. As I felt myself slide off the couch, I heard Delilah say, "I'm with you until the end."

A smile curled my lips as I let the blackness have its way with me.

⚬⚬⚬

His face rose above me like a specter, a cruel sneer contorting his face, but no matter how hard I struggled against my bonds it didn't change anything. There was no happy ending to this tale, only pain and blood. It was always the same. Still, I couldn't help but fight. It was who I was, bred into me like stubbornness or pride.

So, I fought with everything I had. The sound of crunching bone was satisfying until I felt something wet dripping on my face. Oh, god, his blood was on my face. With renewed effort, I tried to bat him away while swiping at my face with my hand. I had to get it off. I couldn't let it stain my skin.

Terror seized my chest, and my eyes popped open, my lips parting. Only the scream never left me because consciousness took over, and I found myself in a brightly lit room, pinned down by the last man I expected to see.

My body shuddered, and I quit struggling. There was something dripping on me, but it wasn't blood.

Switch's face was directly above mine, water dripping onto me from his hair and beard. His eyes, the cinnamon eyes I loved so much, had missed so much, bore into mine.

"Stel," rumbled from his chest, half tortured whisper, half prayer.

He shifted his weight to one side, releasing his hold on my wrist to stroke the side of my face. His touch was feather light and something inside me cracked even more. I didn't want him touching me like I was fragile, like I was somehow broken.

"Don't," I croaked.

His hand paused over my face. "Don't what?"

"Touch me like that."

He shrank back as if I'd hit him, his hand falling to the bed beside me. "I'm sorry, I heard you, and I..."

"You what," I spit back. "Thought you'd come

in here like nothing ever happened and save poor little broken Stella. That I'd be grateful and fall to my knees in worship? Well, you can just crawl back into whatever hole you came out of because it was only a nightmare. I'm doing just fine, so feel free to leave anytime."

His eyes flashed, but before I could decide what emotion lay in their depths, it was gone. "No."

"What the fuck do you mean no?"

"No. To all of it. I'm not leaving. The next time you get pissed and tell me to fuck off, the farthest I'm going is into the next room, and that's only 'cause I value my nuts. Wherever you are is where I belong, even if that means I have to put up with Hunter twenty-four seven."

The stubborn set of his jaw had me cursing the hope that flared unbidden in my chest, and I had to remind myself that his promises didn't mean shit. They were just words. Men made promises all the time that they had no intention of keeping, and Switch was a man like any other. He'd already let me down once and I wasn't stupid enough to give him the chance to do it again.

He cupped my chin in his large hand, his breath fanning my face, almost as if he wanted me to not only hear his words but to feel them ghosting across my skin. "Stel, you are a wild thing, not some flower to be crushed and forgotten. They can put you in a cage, try to

141

break you, but wild things always find a way to escape. And when you've broken the last of your chains, we'll make them pay. Together."

Switch looked down at me expectantly, wetness soaking through the sheet, the heat of his body reaching me through the blanket that separated us. My body softened against his harder one, melting against him without fear, my nipples pebbling against the T-shirt I wore, and a familiar ache gathering deep in my core.

It felt...wrong. In so many different ways. It was too much, too soon, and a part of me hated him for reminding me of how my body had always reacted to him. He brought to the surface something I thought for sure I'd never feel again. Lust.

This was a disaster on so many levels. A fuck storm of epic proportions that I had to shut down in a hurry. My heart was too fragile to handle the rejection that would surely follow.

So, I did the only sensible thing I could and put as much sting into the words as I could muster. "Talk is cheap, Switch, and like I said before, I'm fine. So, you, and the large dick you have plastered to my thigh, can go bother someone else."

The fucker actually had the nerve to smile, and while he looked like shit, comparatively speaking, that lopsided grin of his still got to me. And that was something I simply couldn't allow. There was only enough room for vengeance now in what was left of my tattered heart.

"And, as I said before, my large dick and I aren't going anywhere. Whenever you're ready to hunt these fuckers down, or if you find yourself with a sudden itch you need scratched, you know where to find us."

CHAPTER 19

SWITCH

Stel's body would heal. She was young, fit, and strong, but no matter what she said, she wasn't "fine." Shit, how could she be?

Stel prided herself on being able to hold her own against any man, and they had proven her wrong in the most brutal fashion. I knew it couldn't have been a fair fight because my girl gave as good as she got, but she'd still had her free will stripped away from her in the end.

That wasn't something she would easily get over or forget. It would leave a lasting scar on her soul, which was something I was very familiar with. My soul was littered with them, and I never wanted her to wind up like me. No matter what it took, what I had to do, I wouldn't allow that fierce spirit of hers to dull.

She'd have her vengeance, even if it was the last thing I ever did. I only hoped it brought her peace because I couldn't think of a person more deserving of it than her. Stel didn't do anything in half measures, and the love she freely bestowed on the select few of us lucky enough to receive it was no exception.

"Was I not clear?"

Hunter's detached voice came from the other side of my bike, and after having the first shower I'd had in several days disturbed by the sound of Stel's terrified moan, I wasn't in the mood for twenty questions.

"I've lost track of all the threats I've had lobbed at me lately, so you'll have to narrow it down."

My general fuck-off demeanor, and the fact I hadn't once looked up at him, wouldn't deter Hunter in the slightest. He had zero shits to give unless it was something that directly affected him.

Then again, that might not be a bad thing. It had been a while since I'd gotten into a street brawl with an opponent as worthy as Hunter. Nothing took the edge off like the threat of death.

"Tell me if this sounds familiar. Mad Dog

brought over some of your clothes, so do both of us a favor and use my shower, because you smell like shit. Do not linger in my space any longer than necessary or cause me any problems. You won't like what happens."

"Fuck off, Hunter. Stel was having a nightmare, and I wasn't about to leave her whimpering and thrashing around on the bed."

"And, what? You thought you'd wake her up by holding her down in nothing but a towel. If I'd have known you were too stupid to live, I would have done the world a favor and killed you a long time ago."

It burned me up something fierce to admit that the unfeeling fucker in front of me had a point. The sight of Stel being carried out of the warehouse, covered in blood, in nothing but Hunter's shirt, would haunt me for the rest of my days. But in the heat of the moment, all I could think about was taking away her pain.

Then she'd finally woken up and that smart mouth of hers had been both a balm for my soul and my undoing. There had always been something about the way she challenged me that simultaneously pissed me off and made my dick hard. Which, of course, she had to fucking call attention to, making the situation worse.

"If that were the case, you would have put a bullet in Cannon rather than cleaning up his messes and hiding the worst of it from Ryder."

As soon as the words left my mouth, I

instantly regretted them. It was a low blow, and we both knew it. Cannon had earned his road name many times over, but it seemed sacrilegious to bring up the man's failings being that he was dead.

When I'd heard they were lowering him into the ground, I hadn't thought twice about it, I'd jumped on my bike, and ridden out. Nobody saw me among the mourners because I didn't want them to. I'd been there to mourn a brother, not cause a scene.

Hunter would prefer I didn't know where his skeletons were buried, let alone that I'd had a hand in helping him cover them up. He could say he'd done it so the club wouldn't have to face any blowback, and sometimes I think he actually believed his own lies, but we'd both done what we had out of loyalty. Neither of us could stand the thought of Ryder paying the price for another man's folly when all he'd ever tried to do was help him.

"I'm going to pretend I didn't hear that, otherwise I'll be tempted to break my promise to Brandy and kill you. She said it would upset Stella, though I can't say I understand her logic. You already did that in the few minutes you were inside the house."

For as long as I'd known Hunter, I'd never heard him sound…put out. About anything. Not even when he was a prospect, and we'd sent him on random shitty errands.

A tiny wrinkle over his left eyebrow disturbed his usual mask of indifference, there one second and gone the next, before his forehead smoothed back out. If I hadn't been looking for it, I would have missed the one moment in time when Hunter actually appeared human.

"Not that I give a fuck either way, outside the general inconvenience of having you both in my personal space." And with that, the moment was gone. Hunter had reverted to his usual cyborg self. "But Brandy is an altogether different matter. One I think we should discuss, considering how deeply she's involved herself in Stella's situation."

"Situation would hardly be the word I'd use to describe my girl being kidnapped and traumatized, but you have my attention, nonetheless, out of respect for your old lady."

Brandy protected Stel with the fierceness of a lion, and while I hated being separated from my girl, I was grateful for her. Stel didn't have many girlfriends, and she desperately needed her help to get through this because I knew fuck all about what she was going through.

"I may have received the invitation to the auction, but Brandy was the one who found Stella, along with the locations of about twenty other safe houses. Now it seems she's taking things a step further by helping Stella and Jules's sister take down the whole damn human trafficking ring. She's escaped notice so far, but we both know it's only a matter of time before these men come looking for the source of our information."

Hunter was right. They'd come for Brandy eventually, and if she recoiled at Tweak's touch, what in the hell was she going to do when a man attacked her? She wasn't a fighter like my Stel, despite the dark energy that swirled around her.

"When I told Stel we'd go after these bastards together, I never imagined she'd drag anyone else into this shit."

"While touching, your modern-day Bonnie and Clyde plan doesn't help me keep Brandy safe."

"Shocking as this may seem," I snapped, springing up on the balls of my feet. "You're being a colossal dicklasaur 'cause you failed to see this shit coming in your crystal balls is what's un-fucking-helpful."

Jesus. Dicklasaur? Crystal balls? Before I completely turned into Ryder's ass, I pulled out a cigarette, shoved it in my mouth, and spoke around it as I lit it.

"Now, how about we cut the shit and work together before one of 'em winds up in the wrong hands?"

"What did you have in mind?"

Hunter didn't have the range of emotions it took to pull off terse, but if he did, that's how he would have sounded.

"For starters, why don't you tell me what you know about the sister."

"Delilah Matthews. Age twenty-two. Mother and father both died in a car crash six years ago. One sibling, Jules Matthews. Worked in a hair salon downtown after graduating from cosmetology school. No boyfriend, no friends. The old lady next door was the one who reported her missing. When I went to her apartment, everything was immaculate except for a layer of crime scene dust."

"If it weren't for her brother, she would have made the perfect target. How in the hell did they miss that shit?"

"Turns out, quite easily. When his connection to the CIA didn't turn up in any of my searches, I asked Marco to look into it. He called me back about an hour ago to say it's standard CIA protocol to wipe everything when an agent goes undercover."

"Since when do we have an in with the CIA?"

"We don't," he intoned. "The cartel does."

"Ah." I knew the way our new prospect spoke seemed oddly familiar. To have that kind of clout, he must be a close relative of Valentina's. "Any idea what Jules was working on?"

"That's the part that concerns me." His light eyes scanned my face, giving me the sensation of being a bug burning in the light of his microscope. "He was supposed to bring down Antonio Sanchez, Stella's ex-boyfriend, by any means necessary."

Just when I thought I'd made peace with Stel's newly discovered dating life, somehow it would pop up again like a bad penny and prove me wrong. Every fucking time. It was like I couldn't escape the intangible proof that I'd made a fucking mess of things and placed Stel squarely in harm's way.

"Dirty but clean my ass."

"Hmm. We're missing something here. Possibly a connection between Jules, Antonio, and whoever's behind this human trafficking ring?"

"The sister could be our missing link."

I exhaled a cloud of smoke as I pondered how to gain her trust. With what she'd been through, it wasn't going to be easy. Then the answer came to me, and the beauty of it was, everyone would get what they wanted.

"Stel's going after them no matter what we say or do, and from what you said Brandy will follow Stel's lead, which means so will the sister."

"Are you saying we give the girls free rein?"

"No. I'm suggesting a joint effort between the girls and the club. They share information and agree not to act on it without us, and the club provides the muscle and guns they need to bring down the human trafficking ring."

"What about the girl? How do you propose we get her to talk?"

"Simple," I said, blowing out a cloud of

smoke. "We both know that if she wants to go up against these men and survive, she'll need to learn self-defense and how to shoot a gun. I'll offer to teach her both and have her singing like a canary."

"Let's hope for her sake that you can. Otherwise, we'll have to do things my way, and Ryder's never been fond of my methods."

CHAPTER 20

SWITCH

Stel had unwittingly helped me convince Jules's sister, Delilah, to let me train her when she told the girls that I was "a decent shot." Then, she'd looked over and given me a teasing lopsided smile, shocking the hell out of me. My girl was actually busting my balls. Something she used to enjoy doing on the regular down in the shop. Now, she quickly caught herself, shook it off, turned on her heel, and left the kitchen, but I was still counting it as progress.

One brief unguarded moment didn't mean she'd changed her stance on speaking to me, but it gave me a piece of normalcy I could cling to. Besides, Mad Dog wasn't faring any better than me, and he was her father. But Stel was as stubborn as they came, and she never did anything she didn't damn well want to.

Delilah, on the other hand, was an altogether different sort of complicated. Both women came with their own set of challenges, but I think I'd take Stel's stoic silence over Delilah's space cadet episodes.

She often zoned out in the middle of our self-defense training, and I'd spent more time over the last couple of days trying to get her attention than I did anything else. Which didn't bode well for my goal of getting her to talk, considering the girl hadn't said more than ten words to me.

On top of that, my back hurt something fierce from sleeping on Hunter's front porch swing, Stel avoided me, Brandy was about as skittish as a deer, and Hunter didn't even want the girls in his house let alone me. Needless to say, I was frustrated as hell right now, and I didn't have it in me to rein in my temper with Delilah.

"At this rate, you won't live more than a few minutes."

She blinked a few times and looked up at me with that blank stare I found highly disturbing. "That's enough time for me to kill one man."

"Assuming he's right where you think he'll be, he's not surrounded by other men, and you can shoot. We haven't even gotten to that part yet because I'm afraid you'll lose focus and shoot my foot off! Maybe even something more vital if I'm not careful."

I grumbled the last part, thinking of my dick, but I wasn't about to say that in front of her. With what she'd been through, and her habit of zoning out, fuck only knows how she'd react.

"Until I find him, I'll stay close to Stella. You'd never let anything happen to Stella."

"Willing to bank your life on that?" I asked out of curiosity more than anything else.

"Yes," she said in all seriousness, gracefully lowering herself to the grass and drawing her knees into her chest, as if the simple act of standing had become more than she could bear. "I've seen the way you watch her when you think no one else is looking. You're not like other men. While your desire for her is intense, you don't see her as a warm hole, but as a vital piece of yourself, like one might view their limbs or heart."

The girl might not talk much, but when she did, she was fucking insightful. Stel wasn't like my heart though, she was my heart. She was the very air I breathed, and I'd already seen what life was like without her. I'd been nothing but a fucking mess wrapped up in booze and poor decisions.

"Stel would hardly agree with you," I muttered as I plopped down on the grass a little ways away. Standing over her was growing awkward for both of us.

"She's just trying to protect herself," she said from behind the curtain of her long, dark hair.

Her hair ruffled with the breeze but remained a shield between us, which was fine by me as long as she kept talking. This was the most I'd gotten out of her so far, and I wasn't about to waste the opportunity.

"That's fair, considering she was taken because of me."

Her head snapped up, her dark eyes large in her pale face, the emotionless mask she wore momentarily slipping before she wrestled it back into place. "What do you mean?"

What I was about to do was risky. Most people clammed up when you asked them a personal question relating to something they'd rather not talk about. But it wasn't like if she just got up and walked away that I'd know any less than I do now.

"Have you ever fucked up and your loved one ended up paying the price?"

She turned her head toward the house, her hair a black veil between us. Well, fuck. It appeared that sharing hour was over, at least for today. But if she shut me down again, I'd have no choice but to turn her over to Hunter.

My legs were stiff as I shifted my weight, preparing to stand.

"Yes." Her voice was brittle, barely there, and

I stopped, holding my body still, scared to even breathe. A few tense seconds of silence passed before she finally said, "My brother died because I fell in love with the wrong man. Now, tell me why it's your fault Stella was taken."

That was the last thing I expected her to say. No boyfriends, my ass. How the hell had Hunter missed him? The man was known for being able to find anyone or anything, yet he hadn't found Delilah's mystery man. It made me wonder what else we might have gotten wrong.

I'd gone this far down the rabbit hole, so I figured why not have a little informational pillow talk session with Delilah. But I was drawing the line at braiding hair or talking about my feelings. I was a biker, for fuck's sake, not a teenage girl at a slumber party.

"The short version is Stel told me to fuck off, so I stayed gone, and she found herself plunged straight into hell for the sake of my wounded pride. Now, she can't stand the sight of me, not that I blame her. Some days I can't stand the sight that greets me in the mirror, either. Your turn. Tell me what this man has to do with your brother's death."

Her hair covered the side of her face that I could see, so I had no idea what she was thinking, or if she'd say anything else. The last time she dropped a bomb I almost missed it because I was too quick to walk away. Even though my ass hurt, and I had a crick in my neck,

I was gonna sit here until the cows came home if that's what it took to get her to open up.

Hell, I figured if I could wait out Stel's stubborn ass, then Delilah should be a piece of cake. I pulled out my cigarettes and lighter, prepared to settle in and chain smoke my way to information. She didn't make me wait long before her reedy voice drifted to me on the afternoon breeze.

"He said we needed to keep our relationship a secret because of his work, so I did. Most women would find that suspicious, but since my brother couldn't tell me about his job, I didn't think anything of it. Everything was fine until one night, on the way to dinner, he said he had to stop by work and pick something up. I can't believe I was actually excited. Then he turned down a dirt road and stopped beside an abandoned barn. I thought he brought me there to kill me. You have no idea how many times I've sat in a cell and wished I'd been right."

Her hair shifted, sliding over her shoulder like black silk, her pale cheek now visible. "My brother died because he poked his nose in places he shouldn't have. He'd be alive right now if he'd have just let me go."

Damn. She'd been betrayed in the worst way possible and lost her brother because of it. No words I could ever say would make that right. All I could do now was prepare her for the road ahead. When the time came for us to move on these men, I would do my level best to make sure she lived long enough to see justice done. It would be up to her whether she decided to take out one man or twenty.

"Those weren't men that did those things to you, they were animals, and we will slaughter them like animals."

CHAPTER 21

STELLA

Switch was on a mission, and Delilah had become his new pet project. They were out back for an hour yesterday, mostly sitting on the grass and talking, and today they'd been going at it for the last two hours.

A fine sheen of sweat now coated Switch's arms, neck, and face, and damn if I didn't want to lick it off. Why did his white T-shirt have to cling to his broad shoulders and showcase the hard slabs of muscle lining his stomach? Maybe men were onto something with this wet T-shirt contest business.

I should be enjoying the view, not obsessing about how many times he'd had to lean over Delilah to reposition her arms. But jealousy was a beast I couldn't seem to escape, at least not where Switch was concerned.

For Christ's sake, there wasn't even anything sexual about the way he taught her to defend herself. His lips moved before he reached for her every time, he only touched her when it was absolutely necessary, then he'd quickly drop his hands, and back away. The care and respect he showed for what she'd been through should have warmed my heart, not burned my gut.

Every time his skin touched hers, though, I wanted to stomp over there and yank her away from him by the hair. Yup, I was a special kinda wrong or going straight to hell. Who the fuck knew, maybe both.

"Why don't you join them?" Brandy suggested from behind me.

Shit. She'd caught me staring. Switch and his stupid muscles distracted me when I got up to refill my glass. The sad part was I had no idea how long I'd been staring out the window for. Double shit, the glass in my hand was still empty.

"Nah. I need to finish going through those mugshots."

Hopefully, she'd take the hint and shut up about my momentary lapse in sanity.

"You already recognized one of them this

morning, so it shouldn't be too hard to find the rest. These idiots are all probably friends on social media, anyway. Go."

No such luck. She'd pounced on that shit like a cheetah on a rabbit.

"You've been doing all the hard work, which I love you for, by the way, so the least I can do is make myself useful while I keep you company."

Before I could become distracted again by my hormones, or the jealousy they seemed to cause, I turned away from the window and refilled my glass.

Right now, my hormones and I were at war, and I wasn't sure who was going to win. How could I have nightmares about one man and then turn around the next day and be rubbing my legs together for another? If you asked me, that shit wasn't normal. But then again, I'd never been much of a rule follower. I mean, I hadn't exactly grown up with an accountant for a father.

"Remember when you told me not to get dickmatized and wind up like you?"

"That sounds like something I'd say." I plopped back down in my chair and looked over at her. "Though, I'm still not sure why you didn't take such solid advice. I still maintain that a rabbit vibrator might not be as pretty as that nine-inch dick you're fond of riding, but it'll still get the job done. And a rabbit won't cause you any problems."

How I'd missed fucking with her and watching her turn that adorable shade of pink. The thought that if things had been different, and they hadn't found me in time, that I might never have seen her blush again hit me like a ton of bricks. My stomach did a flip, and I gulped down some water hoping everything would stay where it was supposed to.

"Are you okay?" She cocked her head to the side, her golden eyes assessing me. "You got this faraway look on your face and then you got really pale."

"Sure." I shook off my disturbing thoughts and plastered on a smile. "Why wouldn't I be? We were talking about nine-inch dicks and rabbits."

Her blush went from that cute shade of pink to more of a nuclear red. "Yes, well, I was going to say that since you've already felt the pain from being dickmatized, what's the harm in getting a little something out of it."

She couldn't possibly be suggesting I fuck Switch. The man who left me. The man who broke my heart. For fuck's sake, she didn't like or trust any man outside of Hunter.

"Have you lost your fucking mind?"

"Hear me out." She held up her hands in surrender. "The man obviously wants you. Why else would he be spending his nights on my porch swing. You must still want him since you've had your face pressed against my window, drooling, for the last ten minutes. You have the chance to go back and make it worth the pain. So, why don't you?"

Make it worth the pain. That was what I'd made her promise when she refused to listen to my warnings about Hunter. Now the crafty bitch was using my own words against me. Wasn't that some shit. My own best friend. But could she possibly be right?

Switch had already brought my body back to life against my will and offered me the use of his dick. I'd only be taking him up on his offer. If it was even still on the table. We'd been down this road before, and there was too much at stake now for me to become distracted with feelings. That was all it could be, fucking.

"Maybe," I finally mumbled, so she'd quit staring at me.

Her focus returned to the laptop in front of her, which was my cue to stop thinking about Switch's dick and get back to work. With Brandy's help, there was no way I was going to fail. My bestie could rule the world with a couple clicks of her mouse, but I'd settle for taking away the source of these assholes power. Their money.

It was only a matter of time before we traced the muscle back to the brains of the operation. Then these men would pay for what they'd done, and I'd make sure they could never hurt another woman again.

Click. Another stranger, another faceless

name in the crowd. Click. More of the same. Fuck, was this tedious. Click. Click. Click.

The door behind me opened, and I looked over my shoulder, ignoring the image on my screen, my hand hovering over the mouse. Delilah's face was frozen. Her dark eyes were wide, her pupils twin black holes that sucked you in. Her porcelain skin had gone from having a decidedly rosy hue from being outdoors to bleached of all color.

"No."

Who knew so much anguish could be wrapped up in a single word. Switch must have heard it too because his broad shoulders suddenly filled the doorway behind her. His cinnamon eyes met mine, a question in them.

I shook my head and focused back on Delilah's stricken face as I asked, "What is it?"

"My fuckup."

My eyes shot to Switch, understanding lighting his face. He set his hands on her trembling shoulders, physically moving her to the side so he could fit through the door. His boots seemed to echo around the kitchen as he walked toward me, his eyes looking past me.

When I turned around, I came face to face with the man who'd killed Jules.

Switch pointed at my screen as he looked back at Delilah. "You're sure this is him?"

"I'd know his face anywhere."

Her voice sounded hollow, wooden, broken,

and I hadn't even told her that this was the man who'd killed her brother. Shit. Something was off. This was about more than just her recognizing a face from her time in captivity.

My eyes found Delilah again, and she was still right where Switch left her. "Do you know Mateo?"

At least that was what he'd called himself. Who knew if the name he gave me was real, though I suspected that it was.

Switch tensed beside me, his hand wrapping around my biceps, his rough touch lightening me up from the inside out. "Who is he, Stel?"

I blinked up at him, momentarily stunned. His face was all hard angles and lines, his jaw clenched. He hadn't trimmed his beard even though the hair running down the center of his head was slicked back like usual.

Right now, he looked every bit the outlaw biker that he was, beautiful, savage, and dangerous. Not an ounce of kindness anywhere in him. I should have been terrified, or at the very least intimidated, but this rare glimpse into the more ruthless side of his nature only made me crave more. More of his rough touch, more of the raw power he kept tightly leashed, just more.

"Who is he," he demanded again, lightly shaking me by the arm.

"A member of *Los Sepultureros*," Hunter said, making me jump in my seat. He'd always had the ability to move like death itself. Silent, swift, and often taking you by surprise. "The more important question is, what do they have to do with this?"

That was why Mateo had seemed familiar. Los Sepultureros MC, otherwise known as The Gravediggers, were our most hated rivals. They got others to push their product for them, so none of their members ever went to jail, often recruiting kids to distribute to other kids on school property. The Gravediggers didn't care if a mother of three went to jail for twenty-five years or if a kid was on the evening news because he OD'd on a Fentanyl-laced product so long as they made their money.

Still, when did those assholes make the leap from selling drugs to selling women? It didn't make any sense. They were more street gang than highly organized criminals. Not even Mateo, who was obviously higher up the food chain in Los Sepultureros struck me as having what it took to pull off something of this caliber.

"Well," Hunter prompted from my other side, his light eyes dissecting me.

"I didn't know Mateo was a Gravedigger until now. He told me he wanted to prove that The Devil's Deviants weren't nearly as untouchable as we thought we were, then he shot Jules and left him in the cell with me."

From her spot by the door, I heard Delilah make a keening sound. She already knew the details of Jules's death, but that didn't make it any easier to hear a second time. Her loss was still too fresh.

Brandy got up and moved to comfort her, Hunter's pale eyes leaving mine to follow her progress as he dug his cell phone out of his jeans.

"Ryder, we need to call everyone into church. Stella and the girl have ID'd someone from Los Sepultureros."

He listened for a second before pressing a button on his phone without saying goodbye. "Whether you're ready to face the club or not, Stella, Ryder's expecting us at church in twenty minutes."

CHAPTER 22

SWITCH

Stel clung to my back, her hands wrapped tightly around my waist. I hadn't had the privilege of having her plastered against me while the wind teased our clothes, and a hunk of metal carried us across the blacktop because she'd always ridden her own bike. She'd probably kick my ass for even thinking it, but I liked this way better.

It had nothing to do with any male chauvinistic tendencies, I just enjoyed having her hands on me. The way her hands looked across my stomach every time I chanced a look down made the sluggish organ in my chest beat to life. Her heat filled me to near bursting, and after having been lifeless and cold for so long it felt invigorating. Something like stepping out of a cave and feeling the scorching sun beating down on you.

She still hadn't said much, but then she hadn't protested either when I'd asked her to ride with me. Often, I'd wondered if her fiery nature just wouldn't allow her to concede anything, even something small, and that was why she always fought so hard. If I were being honest, I enjoyed the fight a little too much.

Stel didn't make anything easy, which made her a challenge, and there was nothing I loved more than a challenge. Winning a woman like Stel, one who made you work for it, was worth more to me than bedding a thousand women.

Not that I would know, that was more Tweak's field of expertise. He was the guy women tripped all over themselves to talk to, and I was infinitely glad Stel had never been one of them. I liked him too much to have to worry about killing him. Not to mention things would get real awkward between Ryder and me, being that they were cousins.

Far too soon, we pulled up to the clubhouse, a brick building that spanned an entire city block. The black garage door rolled up for Hunter and we both pulled in behind him, our engines loudly echoing around the small space reserved for club use. Judging by the number of bikes already parked beside the stairs, we were the last to arrive.

Stel swung her leg off, and I immediately missed having her close to me. It was akin to an icy wind making its way inside your coat in the winter. Funny what could change during the span of a ride. Now, I was more determined than ever to make her mine, to tie her to me in every way a woman could be tied to a man.

She walked ahead of me up the metal and wood floating steps, her hand trailing along the whitewashed brick. Her step faltered at the collage of pictures her dad put on the wall, but she shook it off and kept going.

Inside, Hunter breezed past the bar, but as soon as Cherry caught sight of Stel, she squealed. Honest to god squealed, and damn if it wasn't shrill. Cherry was the only grown woman I knew of who could pull that off without you wanting to punch her.

Stel put her finger in her ear and worked her jaw, which Cherry ignored as she hopped over the bar like a gazelle and came running straight for Stel. My hand automatically reached out to steady Stel as hurricane Cherry hit, landing at the small of her back. For such a petite thing, Cherry sure could pack a wallop.

Stel looked over her shoulder at me and raised an eyebrow, so I let my hand drop and moved around them. Neither needed me lording over the top of them anyhow, but I couldn't help overhearing Stel say they weren't doing any "girly shit" now that she was back.

As I walked into church, I couldn't keep the small smile from tugging at the corner of my lips. My girl was back, more or less.

Ryder nodded at the two metal folding chairs off to the side and asked, "Stel coming?"

"Yeah." I plopped down in the one closest to the door. "Cherry stopped her at the front door."

Ryder rolled his eyes but didn't comment. He knew how Cherry was, and while she was a little too sweet for his tastes, he'd still kept her around all these years as a sweet butt. There was something to be said about a girl loyal enough not to run her mouth, even if she was perkier than a cheerleader on crack.

Stel walked in, her T-shirt falling off her shoulder, and her jeans hanging low on her hips. God, she was beautiful, even if she did give me a hateful look as she sat down beside me.

"You left her to hug all over me!"

I shrugged, glad to have her saying more than a few words to me.

"Shouldn't have given me a fuck off look then."

"You earned that look," she groused, crossing her arms.

The action shoved her full, perky tits up, making my mouth water.

"If you two are done?" Ryder asked, one dark

brow raised.

Everyone stared at us, which was damn unfortunate considering my dick was now half hard. Beast even stroked a hand down his dark beard to hide the smirk he wore.

"Yes," Stel hissed back, eyeballing Beast, who wisely slid his hand under the table to protect his junk. We'd all learned the hard way that Stel was fast as lightning and showed no mercy.

"Fan-fucking-tastic." His wooden gavel came down with a crack against the long table in front of him. "Stella, the club has given you the space you asked for. Unfortunately, now that we know Los Sepultureros was somehow involved in your abduction, privacy is no longer a luxury we can afford. We need you to tell us everything about what happened."

She tensed beside me, and I looked over, studying the side of her face. Her teeth dug into her plump bottom lip, drawing blood. Ryder would never ask her to share the details of any assaults she may have endured at these animals' hands, yet there was something she was stewing about. Something she didn't want to share. But what could she possibly want to keep from the club? From her family?

Her tongue snuck out to soothe the lip she'd been worrying as she inhaled a shaky breath. "Hunter says the man who killed Jules is Los Sepultureros, but he didn't claim any affiliations in front of me. All he said was that he wanted to prove The Devil's Deviants weren't as untouchable as they thought. Up until then, I thought they took me because of Antonio, not the club."

Ryder leaned back in his chair at the head of the table, his dark eyes intent on Stel. "And why would you have been taken because of Antonio?"

"He tried to warn me of a security breach where his enemies got ahold of my identity. But he's a complete control freak, so I figured that was his way of restricting my movements. It wasn't until someone opened fire while I was standing in front of his house that I took him seriously."

"I'm your father, for fuck's sake. Why didn't you tell me?"

Mad Dog had stolen the words out of my head, not the father part, but of telling someone, anyone that she was in danger. I wanted to reach over and shake her for putting herself in harm's way. But I didn't. How could I when I was the reason for all of it? Damn. Talk about regrets swallowing a person whole.

"When Antonio and I started dating, I thought he was just a successful businessman. By the time I realized what he was involved in, it was too late for me to leave. I knew too much."

Fuck. She was talking like she was retelling the plot of a blockbuster movie to a friend, factual, and with no emotion. Still, it was like a punch to the gut. Boyfriend. Knew too much.

Too late. The words kept running around and around in my scattered brain.

"Dad, I didn't say anything because I didn't want you getting killed trying to bail me out of the mess I'd made of my life. Losing one parent was bad enough. Besides, Antonio was dealing with the threat."

"Dealing with the threat how?" Mad Dog asked, his voice deceptively low. Whenever he was really pissed, he never yelled. And the quieter he got, the more you needed to consider hauling ass out of his general vicinity.

"Antonio sent his most trusted man to watch me. Jules was never my boyfriend. It was all an act."

For the first time, probably ever, you could have heard a pin drop in church. All eyes were on Stel with the bombshells that just seemed to keep coming out of her mouth.

"Antonio and I both thought his enemies would try for me again, so I stayed out of the public eye, safe at home with Jules. But there wasn't another attempt on my life, and I couldn't hide forever, so we gave them the perfect opportunity at Antonio's club. I don't know what happened to the additional security he hired for the night. Jules was the only one there."

She stared down at her hands as she said, "So, they drugged and took him, same as me."

"Do you know why they didn't just leave Jules there?" Ryder asked, scrubbing a hand down his face.

It was the same question I'd been grappling with for a while.

Stel never looked up, her body rigid in the seat beside me. "No, but they questioned Jules. The only thing he could tell them about the club was that Tweak watched me like a hawk. When I laughed and said that he watched every girl with a pulse, Mateo said he no longer needed Jules and shot him."

She grew quiet after that, and I gently nudged her knee with mine as I asked, "What happened then?"

"They left him to rot in my cell, hoping that would make me more docile. When that didn't work, they took me to a new location. It was there I saw Delilah and knew she looked too much like Jules for them not to be related. That's why I asked Hunter to bring her with us. I couldn't stand to leave her behind when I'd already gotten her loved one killed with my smart mouth."

"Stel." I cradled her chin in my hand, raising it until she met my eyes. "They were always going to kill him once he'd outlived his usefulness. That isn't on you, that's on them. Trust me. They will get what's coming to them."

Her chin trembled in my grasp, but she nodded.

Ryder cleared his throat. "What exactly is Antonio involved in besides guns?"

"Underground fights, call girls, and gambling, mostly," Stel said, breaking my hold to look over at Ryder. "But the primary source of his income doesn't come from any of those things. He supplies weapons to the Middle East. Rocket launchers, missiles, grenades, guns, you name it, he ships it."

"Jesus," Gunner muttered under his breath.

His time in the deserts of Afghanistan did a number on him, and we were wading into dangerous waters with this subject matter. If the dark look on his face was any indication, Gunner would gladly take out Antonio on Stel's behalf.

"Have you been in contact with Antonio since you've been back?" Ryder asked, his fingers drumming on the tabletop.

The thought she might want to be in contact with one of her old—there was that word again —boyfriends hadn't even occurred to me. Now that it had, my stomach tightened painfully, waiting on her response. If she asked me to let her go, I wasn't sure that I could.

"No," she said, looking over at me as she answered.

My fist unclenched in my lap. Good. There was no way I was letting her get anywhere near that fucker.

"Until we know more, it's probably best if he thinks you're still MIA. For now, at least, you'll have to avoid your apartment, the club, and your bike."

"I get my apartment and the club, but why wouldn't I be able to ride back to Hunter's on my bike?"

"Shit," Tweak muttered from the end of the table. "That's my bad, Stella. If I'd known it was going to be a problem, Ryder and I never would have tried to surprise you."

"Where is my bike?" Stel bit out.

Oh shit. If those boys had fucked with her bike, she was going to lose her shit and burn down the club. Nobody, and I mean nobody, came between Stel and her bike. The bike she and I spent hours working on. The same piece of shit bike her father gave her.

"Down in the garage."

She was out of that folding metal chair so fast she tipped it over, the door banging off the wall with the force she used to open it.

"What the fuck did you guys do?" I asked, afraid of the answer.

"She's going to love it." Tweak waved off her reaction like it was nothing. "Honest. I just wanted to get her out of here so we could discuss what we're going to do about this shitstorm we got brewing. The last thing we need is for her to go all *GI Jane* before we're ready to make a move and wind up getting herself killed."

"Good thinking," Beast said from beside him. "Better we know what we're walking into before we let her loose on those fuckers. And right now, there are too many hens in the henhouse for my tastes."

"Agreed." Ryder's fingers paused in their drumming. "Hunter, how do you know that guy the girls ID'd was with Los Sepultureros?"

"I recognized him from the day we scoped out their old farmhouse. He was inside, watching them bring in the guns and drugs."

"Since when is Los Sepultureros in the business of human trafficking?" I shook out a cigarette but didn't light it. Most of the guys were nonsmokers, and I was their guest, so pinching it between my fingers would have to do. "The man Hunter recognized is the same one that Delilah says brought her to an abandoned barn and left her to be sold."

"And how is any of that connected to Antonio?" Colt shook his head. "'Cause my money is still on that greasy fucker being involved. She was fucking taken at his club with his man watching. Or what he thought was his man."

"What if they aren't directly linked?" I asked, watching the cigarette roll between my fingers. "But they have a common ally or enemy. We still don't know who sent Hunter the email inviting him to the auction."

"Interesting," Hunter hummed. "I think I need to look closer at Antonio. He might actually prove to be a worthy adversary."

Gunner tucked the hair that had fallen into his face back behind his ear. "As long as you don't torture or kill him without me. I owe him for the amount of metal the US government has had to remove from my body because of his greed."

"Not so much of a Boy Scout now are we," the prospect, Marco, purred.

Yup. He might not look like Valentina, but there was no mistaking his accent, the way he carried himself, or the glint in his eye. Now that I was looking for the connection, I could see his resemblance to their father, Miguel. Only, his dark hair was longer and had a wavy curl to it that most women would kill for, and his eyes didn't have the same hint of cruelty.

"Shut the fuck up. You didn't sweat your balls off in a foreign country only to watch your friends dying all around you."

"Enough," Ryder said with a bang of his gavel. He pointed it in Marco's direction. "Make yourself useful and ask Diego to reach out to the CIA. Tell them it's a courtesy call to let them know their asset has been killed and who did it. If they ask how we know, tell them one of our own witnessed it. I want to see if they do anything with that information."

His gavel swung to Hunter. "Do what you do best, and for fuck's sake take Gunner with you. It'll be good for him to work off a little steam."

Hunter inclined his head in Gunner's direction.

"Colt, help Hunter by monitoring who comes and goes from Antonio's club. If you need access to feeds or facial recognition, reach out to Brandy and see what she can do."

"Roger that, Prez."

"Val, Marco, and I will spy on Los Sepultureros and see what they're up to. Dagger and Beast, you guys are to hold down the fort while Pops and Mad Dog take turns watching Hunter's place. If whoever's behind this figures out that we have a hacker and two of their former prisoners, Switch will need help to hold them off until the rest of us get there."

Ryder's gavel came down with a bang. "We'll meet back here in two days."

CHAPTER 23

STELLA

I stood in front of my bike, wiping underneath my eyes with the corner of my T-shirt as I stared down at it. Fuck. Why couldn't I stop crying? This was total bullshit. It was Tweak, that asshole. He had me thinking they did something fucked-up to my baby. Got me all worked up. Then they turned around and blindsided me by actually doing something sweet.

Yeah, that was why I was crying like a baby. 'Cause I got blindsided. If I had been prepared for sweet, everything would have been fine. The waterworks would have remained where they belonged, carefully contained.

She was a real beauty, though. What I could see of her through my tears, anyway. Definitely one of a kind. I could see why Ryder told me I'd have to stay away from her. She was a showpiece everyone would stare at, and by extension, they would see me.

The sides of her wheels and tank reminded me of the sky just before it stormed, which popped against the silver of engine parts, and the black of my tires and exhaust. They painted the center a blue so dark it almost looked black. Both colors were seamlessly blended together with a sparkly topcoat, the flecks of gray in it playing off the blues.

The Devil's Deviants logo sat front and center on my gas tank. I'd always loved their logo. The skull that held the weight of the city atop its head with a raging storm at its back. It was fitting, really. There was always someone looking to take their crown, to topple the grip they had on this city, yet time after time the club only came out of it stronger.

There were some who would always see a criminal when they looked at my dad, but I saw a god. Still did, gray hair, bad hands, and all. He would always be larger than life to me. Maybe it was because he loved his family and his club with a fierceness that could never be matched. He'd stood by his wife until the very end, even when it sapped her energy just to run her hand over his beard. Pops and dad had been together longer than most of the club's members have been alive.

I was proud of him. Well, of Pops and Dagger too. They were all that was left of the original members. Hell, I wanted to be them when I grew up, not doing dumb shit that put them all in danger. And for what? To forget about the man who'd broken my heart.

"Fuck," I whispered to my beautiful bike.

"Well, we could, but we might smudge your shiny new paint job."

I jumped, turning around, watching him as he materialized out of the shadows. "You're getting to be almost as creepy as Hunter."

My heart beat double time as he swaggered toward me. Yes, swaggered. His arrogant stride was as effortless as it was sexy. Honestly, how could a man look that hot in a pair of low-slung jeans, a white T-shirt, and a cut?

"Nah," he said, his deep voice hitting me right in the pussy. Damn him and the chrome stallion he rode in on. "Nobody's as creepy as that fucker. I was trying to decide whether I should wait to see if I'd get the pleasure of watching you straddle her. You know, seeing as how you can't ride her."

He stopped in front of me, his large hands cradling my face as I looked up at him. His brow furrowed, and he wiped underneath my eyes with both of his thumbs.

"Stel, I swear, I'll kick both their asses if you're upset about what they did to your baby."

It took me a second to respond because his chest was a hairsbreadth away from my nose, and his thumbs were practically massaging my face. Who knew that could send electric sparks down my body? It was my face, for Christ's sake. My face.

"What? No, it's beautiful."

His cinnamon eyes roamed over my face, searching. For what, I wasn't sure.

"A few tears don't make you any less of a badass, Stel. You're still the strongest person I've ever known."

Well, fuck. He'd now seen my tears, wiped them away with a tender touch, and called me a badass in the space of a few minutes. Between all that, and the way he was devouring me with his eyes, I wasn't sure anymore which end was up. And that was before he slid his hands into my hair, wrapping it around his fist, and tugged on the strands.

He was going to ruin me at the rate we were going, yet I was helpless to stop him. Like it or not, I was a junkie for Switch. Just a hit, a taste, and I was a goner.

"But now that I have your attention, we're alone, and you're actually speaking to me, there are a few things I'd like to clear up. The other day, when you woke up, I wasn't gentle with you because I thought you were broken. I was gentle with you because I missed you so much it physically hurt, and I wanted to be. For me, not you. Understand?"

I nodded my head in his hold, grateful that he'd carefully avoided mentioning my nightmare. Even in front of Switch, or maybe especially in front of him, I never wanted to be seen as weak. Because who wanted a partner that couldn't carry half the load, and in our world, the burden of that weight crushed the weak.

"Sometimes you make me crazy, and I can't decide whether to turn you over my knee and tan your ass or fuck you senseless. You're the only woman I've ever known who can look sexy as fuck in a pair of coveralls painting a car, then show up in the clubhouse in a tiny dress and boots. That day you had me so damn frustrated because I'd already jacked off twice in the garage's bathroom and I still wanted to fuck you up against the bar."

Holy shit. He certainly had a funny way of showing it. He was a total asshole that night. I ended up hiding out in Colt's room, mainly because I was tipsy, and it was the only one that was unoccupied. When he found me there later, curled up on his bed, playing *Candy Crush*, I expected him to kick me out. Instead, he kept me company until I sobered up enough to go home. Of course, that was when Switch found me.

"The thing that always kept me from having what I wanted was your father. He took me in, kept me from going to jail, and it just didn't seem right to repay his kindness by tarnishing his only daughter. But I'm a jealous asshole, and I had it in my head that if I couldn't have you, then nobody else would either."

His brow furrowed, and his lips turned down in the corners. I sucked in a breath, preparing myself for what he may say next.

"Over time, though, you began to pull away. We laughed less and fought more. It was either tell you how I felt, and pray Mad Dog would forgive me, or lose you forever. Only, you took one look at my grand gesture, my boombox in the pouring rain underneath your window moment and told me to fuck off. Not gonna lie, that shit hurt, but continuing to see you every day, knowing that you sent me away, fucked with my head. Bad. So, I packed a bag and transferred charters."

His hands fisted my hair tighter and I couldn't help the moan that escaped my lips. "When Ryder told me you'd been taken, I dropped to my knees, too weak to stand. It was then I knew no matter what I did that I'd never be able to quit you. You're in my blood, underneath my skin, a part of my very soul. Wherever you go, I go, even if that's to the grave."

He suddenly released me, my body swaying as he took a step back. "You don't have to believe me. Friendzone me to the end of time. Just don't expect me to leave or allow another man to touch you because that ain't happening."

Friendzone him? Was he freaking kidding me with that shit right now? We were way past that. Switch had dickmatized me a long time ago, and he'd been either making my heartbeat faster or tearing it apart ever since.

Brandy had been right. There was nothing left of me for him to hurt, and I had yet to do anything beyond sneak a peek at his dick. Which was a damn shame.

Fuck if it was still too soon or not. Fuck what I should or shouldn't be feeling. Boris wasn't stealing this moment from me. He'd lived inside my head for long enough, and it was time for me to evict his ass. I was going to do whatever the hell I wanted from now on, starting with jumping Switch.

He caught me in his arms, his large hands cradling and then squeezing my ass, even as he stepped back from the force. I grabbed his face in both hands and leaned in. Our lips met, little tingles starting at my scalp and working their way down my body. The kiss was frenzied, tongues twisting, and teeth gnashing.

My hands roamed over the bulging muscles of his arms as they flexed and twisted from holding me up. Vaguely, it registered that we were moving, but the breath exploded from my lungs when my back hit metal. He shifted so he could support me in one hand while the other tore at the bottom of my T-shirt.

Holding on to his shoulders, I leaned forward, and he broke the kiss long enough to rip my shirt free and throw it off to the side. The metal at my back was cold, and dug into my back, but I didn't give a fuck because Switch's lips were on mine and his deft fingers were releasing the fasteners on my bra.

He threw that off to the side as well, breaking the kiss again to stare down at me.

"Fucking beautiful," he murmured before bending his head to take one of my nipples into his mouth.

He sucked loudly, almost lewdly, and it was as if there was a connection between my nipple and my pussy because I felt the moist material of my panties clinging to my skin. My hips gyrated, the bulge behind his zipper giving me the friction I desperately needed.

Fire. It felt like my skin was on fire everywhere, the heat licking its way down my spine.

It wasn't enough; I needed to be closer, flesh to flesh. The leather of his cut was soft against my fingertips as I pushed it down his arms, a frustrated sound welling from deep within his chest as he had to shift to accommodate my request.

He let my nipple go with a wet pop, his eyes following the motion of my tits before his head disappeared long enough to shed his T-shirt. It, too, went flying somewhere.

My eyes ate up the visible parts of his chest and stomach. Black ink covered every slab of muscle. My hands followed the path my eyes had taken, my short nails clawing over the angel wings on the swell of his pecs before dipping down to explore the coiled serpent over the ridges of his stomach.

A groan vibrated the flesh under my fingertips, and he shifted me again, his large hand going to work on the button and zipper of my jeans. I liked where his head was at, our arms intertwining as I reached down to tug at his belt, our hungry mouths finding each other again. A symphony of grunts and moans filled the garage, and I'd never heard anything half as sexy.

His hand slid into the back of my jeans, one finger sliding down the length of my thong before he squeezed my ass again. His needy groan as his other hand shoved and pushed at my jeans in frustration hit something deep inside of me, bringing the old Stella back to the surface. The brash girl who fearlessly took life by the balls and didn't give a shit what anyone thought. Maybe she wasn't dead after all, just buried.

My legs uncurled from around his waist, my boots hitting the concrete floor with a thud. He kept one hand glued to my ass but made quick work of yanking down my jeans and thong while

I stepped out of my boots.

He lifted me again, the tool chest at my back rattling as he leaned me back against it, my legs winding back around his waist. The cool of the metal only highlighted how heated my skin was.

His lips devoured mine, his chest rubbing against my tender nipples creating delicious ripples of sensation. I rubbed myself up and down his body like a cat in heat, wanting to be closer. His jeans were open, but not off, part of the material course and part of it soft. The sensation, while pleasurable, was driving me crazy.

My nails dragged down the skulls on his arms, eliciting a low growl, as I wiggled against him, using both of my feet and my hand to shove his jeans down. His cock sprang free, slapping against my ass, an animalistic noise ripping free from my throat.

He grunted into the kiss, one of his hands leaving my ass to notch his dick against my entrance. The head slipped inside, stretching me, little zings of pleasure curling down my spine. Fuck yes. Finally.

Only he stopped. Everything. His lips stilled on mine, his body shaking with the effort of holding himself still.

I broke the kiss and leaned my head back to have a look at him. His face was slack, almost blissful, his eyes closed. I'd never seen him look this peaceful, which was good, but it didn't help the pressure building in my core. At the moment, I was a broken furnace, dying to explode and take the whole place down with me.

"Switch, if you don't fuck me right this second, I'm going to kick your ass."

He groaned, "Can't a man take a second to enjoy the best pussy god ever created?"

Well, when he put it like that, how could I not? He'd already crushed most of the worries I had about having sex again. I guess I could wait an extra minute to find out whether I'd still be able to have an orgasm. Didn't mean I was happy about it, though.

His eyes fluttered open, his irises more of a dark whiskey than cinnamon. He stared back, his arm muscles flexing beneath my fingertips as he impaled me on his thick cock in one go. The stretch perfectly combined pleasure and pain, my nails digging into his heavily tattooed skin to anchor myself. He slid almost all the way out before thrusting back in, a porn-worthy moan tearing up my throat.

Every time he slid deep inside me the rough hair at the stem of his dick rubbed against my pussy, teasing my clit. The force of his thrusts rattled the tools in the chest behind me, his balls slapping against my ass. The mingling sounds were like a dirty symphony, playing to my pussy and hitting all the right notes.

Now that he'd had his moment, he wasn't holding anything back. This was fucking, pure and simple. It was loud, obscene, wild, and utterly perfect. Higher and higher he took me with each stroke of his cock, and when I broke apart, tears sprang from the corners of my eyes.

It was the freest I'd ever been. Nothing could compare, not even racing over the blacktop on my baby.

He didn't stop either; he fucked me through it, a second orgasm hitting me even harder than the first. My choked scream echoed off the walls of the garage, mixing with his grunts of pleasure. I slid my hands up his arms and around his shoulders, sinking my fingers into the soft longer strands of hair at the center of his scalp.

"Yes," he moaned as I licked the sweat from his neck.

The salty tang of his skin was its own aphrodisiac, bringing on yet another orgasm, my fingers pulling at his hair with the force of it.

With one last hard thrust, he shouted, "Fuck!"

He spilled inside of me, his body shuddering with the force of it. He panted into my neck, his warm breath giving me the chills. We were wrapped up in each other, connected as two people could possibly be.

My heartbeat was loud inside my head. I'd been a fool to think I could fuck one man to forget another. There was no coming back from this. Switch had tightened the last chain. I'd been wrong. So, so, wrong. This time when he left it wouldn't just hurt, it would shatter me into a thousand unrecognizable pieces.

CHAPTER 24

STELLA

Brandy and Hunter's place had become my home away from home. A place for me to lick my wounds while I healed. Nobody wanted or expected anything from me here. Well, except for maybe Hunter, but staying away from his room, and out of his way, was surprisingly easy.

If only the same could be said for Switch. Apparently, he took my fucking him to mean he would be sharing my bed. I woke up in the middle of the night, little spoon to his big spoon, a very obvious part of him digging into my lower back.

Once my panic attack subsided, I tried to turn over, ready to light into him, only to have him tighten his grip.

His breath was hot against my ear, sending shivers down my spine, as he'd mumbled, "Just a few more minutes, Stel."

As his soft snore ruffled my hair, I remembered he'd been sleeping on the porch swing. So, I took pity on him and let him stay. But at first light, I ninja'd myself out of his hold and went in search of a shower and coffee.

It was better for both of us if he didn't get too comfortable. Before I could think about Switch as anything other than a fuck buddy, I needed to finish this. For myself, for my family, and for all the other women still being held hostage by those assholes.

Which was why Brandy and I were sitting in front of our laptops at her kitchen table. She was doing whatever the hell it was super genius computer nerds did while I clicked through more mugshots. Only this afternoon, I had help in the form of a silent shadow breathing down my neck.

Switch had moved on from self-defense to shooting, and now that Delilah could hit the broad side of a barn, she thought she was *Lara Croft* or something. If Delilah went after these men on her own, she wouldn't last a minute.

Switch was right to help her, I just didn't want her thinking she was invincible now that she'd learned a few moves. These men didn't fight fair, and knowing how to fight and shoot hadn't helped me. She would need to outsmart them.

Click. Click. Click.

"Wait, go back. That guy looked familiar."

Click. Well, I'll be damned. How the hell had I missed old Carrot Top? I pressed the print button. Maybe Switch was right to get her all fired up. I'd just have a chat with her later about never underestimating your opponent.

"I don't believe it," Brandy said breathlessly, sitting back in her chair, and staring at her screen.

"Okay, genius, we give up," I teased her. "Found all the safe houses? The man behind all this shit? Honestly, I could go either way given your skill set."

She looked over at me, a small smile teasing the corner of her lip. "Not yet, smartass, but I found out who sent Hunter that email. It took me a while to get past all the layers of encryption, but it came from the CIA."

"You're sure?"

"Yup. More specifically, from Martin Johns over at the CIA. Jules must have asked him to send it for him because he didn't want to risk blowing his cover."

What I didn't want to tell Brandy, especially in front of Delilah, was that Jules being the sender of that email actually made perfect sense.

He knew what he was risking when he let those men take us, and if they killed him, he needed a way to get me out of the mess he'd gotten me into. He must have sent that invitation to Hunter as a backup plan and thank fuck he did.

I moved to stand behind her, Delilah following me. "Do you have a way of hacking into Martin Johns's email?"

"Hypothetically speaking, now that I have his IP address, I could use it to test the ports until I found one that let me into his computer. But I have a strict policy of finding out why I'm committing a felony before I actually do it."

"Now who's the smartass, huh," I said with a smack to her shoulder. "Jules wouldn't have communicated with this guy via email from the field, but it's possible this guy forwarded any updates Jules gave him to a superior via email."

"Gotcha, you want to check his sent items folder to find out what Jules knew."

She started pounding away on her keyboard. Damn, I loved this girl. It's not just any friend who would commit a felony for you.

A screen within her screen popped up, and it all looked like gibberish to me. Everyone should be scared. My bestie could totally take over the world if she wanted to.

Something beeped, and then I was staring at this guy's email. Hot damn! We looked over Brandy's shoulder as she scrolled through his sent folder. After a few minutes, she stopped and clicked on one to enlarge it.

"Looks like it's a list of names of people Antonio did business with."

"Can you screenshot it or something?"

"I'll do you one better." A second later, I heard the printer whirring, and she looked down at her watch. "Better get out of his email before someone figures out that they've been breached. We can always hack into their system again later if this list doesn't pan out."

"Did I ever tell you I fucking love you?"

"No, but the feeling is mutual."

I picked up the paper off the printer and started scanning through the names. Most of the people on this list I recognized from my time with Antonio and quickly dismissed, but that still left five names. It shouldn't take too long to check these people out.

Wait, damn, I didn't have my bike. What in the hell was I going to do now? It wouldn't do any good to send to Hunter because it's not like he'd recognize any of these people. I suppose he could text me photos but fuck that. I'd been cooped up here looking at mugshots practically since I came back, and this was something that only I could do.

If I had to ride with someone, which by the way I hated, I'd much rather it be Switch than Hunter. Now, all I had to do was find him and talk him into it.

CHAPTER 25

SWITCH

Stel was already mentally pulling away from me and shoring up her defenses before I'd even slipped my dick out of her. Fuck that. She wasn't getting away that easily. Not after I finally had her the way I'd always wanted, and it was beyond anything I could have ever envisioned.

She was wild, uninhibited, and sexy as hell. And her pussy. OH, MY DAMN. Her pussy squeezed my cock so hard every time she came that I damn near saw stars.

Fuck giving that up. Hell to the no. I'd had a taste and now I wanted more. So much more. I wanted to spend my life fucking her any place, any time of the day or night, that she'd let me.

She could fight me all she wanted, but she was going to be my old lady. I didn't care if I had to hogtie her to my bed, she was falling asleep in my arms every damn night. End of story.

But Stel wasn't going to just climb into my bed and stay put. Oh, no. She was like the stray cat you had to coax to your side with yummy tuna or she'd claw your eyes out. And right now, Stel's tuna was vengeance.

Which was fine, she more than deserved it, but I was going to make her give me something in return. She was none too happy about my little condition, either. Well, join the club. I wasn't happy when I woke up in her bed, alone, and with a hard dick to boot.

Riding around with her on the back of my bike wasn't a hardship, it was a claiming of sorts, a way of letting everyone know she was mine. Every time my bike rolled to a stop, I itched to put my hands on her, adding to my claim, but I refrained. Barely. Now wasn't the time for that.

I didn't hold out hope that any of the names on her list would pan out, but I wasn't about to let my guard down. For all I knew, the men who took Stel, or Antonio, might be combing the streets looking for her. We needed to maintain a low profile and be quick about our surveillance.

The first name on her list belonged to Gerald Moore. He lived on a sprawling ranch with a giant metal gate, complete with a horseshoe above it. We hadn't been invited to his daughter's sweet sixteen, so we had to spy on the festivities from behind the back end of a Range Rover parked beside the house. Stel's eyes scanned all the male party goers, but she shook her head at me, a pretty pout on her face.

Our next stop was an Italian restaurant owned by Lorenzo Castellano. We sat in a booth in the back, sharing the best tiramisu I'd ever had in my life. If I had to kill him, I was definitely torturing him for the recipe for this shit first. The waitress stopped by to ask if we needed anything else, and Stel struck up a conversation with her.

Stel might not make friends easily, or be a girly girl, but she sure could weasel information out of a person. Most of the time without them even knowing it. So, I sat back, sipping an espresso, watching her do her thing. It was a hell of a turn on. By the time the waitress walked away, I considered taking Stel into the bathroom and fucking her.

She claimed she was going to the restroom, which fit in with my plans perfectly, but when I went to slide out after her, she shook her head and walked away. Damn. Now I was stuck in this booth with jeans that were too tight in the crotch. I shoulda paid closer attention to their conversation, so I'd know if she was really going to the bathroom or if she was spying.

Hell. I better sit tight for a few minutes. If I fucked up Stel's chance at seeing this guy by going back there, she was liable to kick me right in the dick. And a bruised dick was the last thing I needed when I actually stood a chance of getting with my girl.

She came back to our table with its checkered tablecloth and candle in the center and shook her head. At least I'd made the right call. Throwing down a couple of twenties, I adjusted the front of my jeans and followed her out of the restaurant.

The next guy on our list lived in one of the few high-end apartment buildings in town. It had a brick exterior with a four-story parking garage attached to it. Honestly, I had always hated parking garages. It was guaranteed to be dark no matter if it was noon or midnight, and there were too many places a person could hide. If I could, I avoided them.

But not today. I drove my bike slowly through the levels like I belonged here and then took my time backing into a space beside a large SUV.

When I killed the engine, I looked back at Stel. "What now?"

"We wait."

She seemed so sure, yet I felt compelled to point out, "There are three other levels. He could come or go from another one and we'd miss him. We could be sitting here awhile."

She raised a brow. "Have somewhere else to be?"

"Not particularly," I said with a sigh, knowing she had me there.

We had a clear view of the only elevator, yet thanks to the SUV beside us, we couldn't easily be seen. From our vantage point, we could see any cars coming up the ramp, but they wouldn't see us until they made the turn to park. The only negative to our hiding spot was that should an unexpected variable arise, we were effectively backed into a corner.

For a while we sat in silence, her breath fanning the back of my neck. Restless energy thrummed through my body and after only thirty minutes I couldn't take it anymore.

I stood, carefully extracted my leg, so I didn't disturb Stel, at least not yet anyway, and stretched. Her eyes followed the line of my body, stopping at my waist where there was a gap between my T-shirt and my belt.

"W...what do you think you're doing?"

"Stretching. But now that you mention it, this stop is a little boring. Up for a game of truth or dare?"

We'd played this game as kids and Stel had never been able to resist a dare. Back then it was shit like I dare you to steal one of your dad's cigarettes. Now, I had something entirely different in mind.

"What the hell," she said, swinging her leg

over my bike. "Truth or dare?"

The lighting was dim, but I could see the same restless energy thrumming underneath her skin as she stretched.

"Truth."

Stel knew I always picked truth, so I wasn't even sure why she asked. My old man used to say, "A good horse never changes their stall." There wasn't much he taught me worth a shit, but for some reason I'd held on to that little nugget.

"Why did you break Derek Hughes's arm in high school?"

She was coming out swinging today I see. This one fell under the category of not one of my proudest moments.

"I was powerless to take your virginity, but I'd be damned if I let some high school quarterback have it in the back seat of his car. I've never pretended to be a good man, and with you, there's no line I won't cross." Since we were apparently being formal about this shit, I asked, "Truth or dare?"

She cocked a hip out. "Dare."

"I dare you to kiss me."

My eyes ate up what I could of her in the dim light as she strutted over to me like she was hot shit. I waited until she was on her tiptoes, her lips almost meeting mine, but not quite, before I spoke.

"I didn't say where yet, now did I?"

Her breath fanned my face as she huffed, "If

you say your dick, I'm biting it after I kiss it."

Damn, I loved that smart mouth of hers.

"I was going to say neck you dirty, dirty girl."

"Asshole," she muttered a second before her lips touched the side of my neck.

I expected her to play hard to get. Give me a peck and then pull away. But not today. She leaned in, peppering little butterfly kisses from my collarbone to my ear. Then I felt her wet tongue trace her way back down. Fuck me and this girl.

"Truth or dare."

Bringing my mouth down to her ear I whispered, "Dare."

For a second, she paused, unsure what to do because I'd never said dare before. Jesus, I hoped she didn't give me anything stupid. Go for sexy, I tried to prod her mentally. Not sure we had that type of connection, but it couldn't hurt.

"I dare you to make me come without fucking me."

Holy shit. It actually worked. And fuck if she didn't say it in a breathy tone that went straight to my dick.

"Not a problem."

She let out a little squeak as I lifted her, carrying us deeper into the shadows, leaning her against the cool cement wall. Her tits were eye level and using the wall as leverage I freed one of my hands to tug her T-shirt up. The lace of her bra felt scratchy against my hand, unlike her silky skin.

Her nipple was already hard, pushing against the lace as I pinched it between my thumb and first finger, her gasp echoing around us.

"Shh," I cooed. "Watch over my shoulder and tell me if someone is coming."

My mouth found her other nipple through the lace, my tongue laving it before I gently bit down. Her back arched into me, and I smiled against her tit. This was the best game of truth or dare I'd ever played.

I switched sides, torturing her nipple through the wet lace with my fingers as I sucked on her other one. Back and forth I went, giving each of her nipples the attention they deserved, listening to her shuddered breaths.

"Tell me, Stel," I murmured against the lace. "Are you wet for me?"

"Yes."

Her reply was breathless and begrudgingly torn from her lips like she was fighting her reaction to me and losing. Jesus, this girl was every wet dream I'd ever had come to life.

I delved back into her, getting lost in her vanilla scent that was missing its tinge of gas and paint. It was still her, still utterly mouthwatering, but I lamented its loss, nonetheless. Her little nails scraped against the back of my skull, drawing my focus away from what was missing and reeling me back in.

Happily, greedily, I feasted on her lace

covered flesh until I felt her body shake in my hold. When I lifted my head, I only lifted it enough to bury my nose in her neck. Her pulse beat wildly, and her chest rose and fell in rapid succession. No matter how many times she came undone for me it was never enough. I always wanted more.

She slid down my body so I could set her on her feet, my hand sliding inside the front of her jeans. When I reached her pussy, the material covering it was soaked. My thumb rubbed against her lace covered clit while another finger pushed aside her panties enough to enter her.

She held on to my forearms as I fucked her with my finger, her arousal coating my fingers. A choked gasp left her, like she couldn't hold it back, her body tightening around me. She was close again, but I wanted her to come on my dick, not on my hand. The cutest little whimper echoed around us when I slid my finger out of her.

I pressed my lips against her ear, my hands already undoing the button on her jeans. "Don't worry, Wild Thing, this time I'm going to make you come so hard that my balls will be drenched."

Her breathing was harsh, her whispered words filled with that glorious rasp I'd been missing. "Wild Thing?"

I suppressed a smile as I slid her jeans over her ass. "That's what you are."

When I reached her thighs, I bent down and unlaced one of her boots, sliding both it and her jeans off that leg. My hands slid back up her legs as I stood, grabbing that luscious ass of hers in both hands, and lifting her.

"Beautiful and unrestrained with tiny claws you've sunk deep into my heart," I panted, walking us behind the SUV. Using the wall to steady her, I slid my jeans down to my knees. "Now, my Wild Thing," I whispered as I notched myself at her entrance. "Eyes over my shoulder the whole time and tap me twice if I need to stop."

Fuck, I hoped my luck held out and nobody came before we did. My balls were near to bursting and I couldn't wait to spill into her tight heat.

Her thighs tightened around me as I plunged into her sweet pussy. My head swam, the sensation almost overwhelming me. After taking a second to recover, I bounced her up and down on my cock, my hands digging into the bottom of her ass. My Wild Thing lived up to her name, digging her little nails into my shoulders, hard. Fuck, yeah.

While she watched our surroundings, I buried my head in her neck. If I could, I'd crawl inside this girl and stay there. I wanted her to give me hell, then turn around and take my cock. She was mine, and I wanted every fucker out there to know it.

So, I licked and sucked in the spot where her neck met her shoulder over and over as I fucked her. Those little nails of hers scratched and clawed at me as she came, the start of a moan escaping before she could hold it back. Fuck how I wished she could holler the whole place down. For now, though, I'd settle for her drenching me with the force of her orgasm.

Every time I slid out of her, her pussy clamped down around me, trying to suck me back in. The obscenely wet slapping sounds of our fucking echoed around us, spurring me on. I wanted to make her come once more before I did, and I was damn close to losing it.

Only Stel could make me lose control, unravel me so completely I didn't have a fucking clue where I ended, and she began.

Her pussy contracted around me as she came, her nails dug into my biceps, her pussy milking my cock dry as I exploded inside of her. Both of us shook with the force of it, our chests heaving in sync. Our breathing sounded loud in the darkened alcove as she tensed in my arms, her hand frantically tapping my shoulder.

Fuck. I lowered her to the ground and rushed to help her with her pants and boot before sliding my own jeans up and zipping them. By the time the car rounded the curve, we were both dressed and hiding behind the SUV, her harsh breathing the only evidence of what we'd been doing.

A *Corvette* whipped into the spot across from us, its engine dying as the elevator across from it dinged. Both the car door and the elevator door opened at the same time. Inside the elevator was well lit and I heard Stel's intake of breath as the fat, old fucker inside stepped out.

In the gloom, all I could make out of the guy who exited the sports car was his build. He was tall and athletic, his swagger that of a younger man. They met each other halfway and stopped, the younger man dwarfing the older one, yet he bent his head in deference.

"Well?" the older guy asked.

"Nothing yet, boss. It's like she just vanished."

"Jesus, what do I pay you for? Never mind. I'll take care of it myself."

The older guy tottered away, a black Lincoln Town Car's lights flashing as the doors unlocked. The tall guy shook his head, watching his boss slowly back out before he turned around and went back to his sports car.

Stel left my side before I could grab her, swiftly moving toward the guy's sports car. What in the fuck was she doing?

He opened his door, his back thankfully to us as we approached. A faint shaft of light caught the glint of steel in Stel's hand a second before she made her move. Even though I was only a few steps behind her, there was nothing I could do to stop what happened next had I wanted to.

She plunged the blade into the side of his neck, a gurgled moan escaping him as he fell backward into Stel.

Catching him, she twisted the blade, hissing, "You don't deserve a quick death. But today's your lucky day, asshole, because that's all I have time for."

Holy shit. I watched, dumbfounded, as her arms enveloped him, her hands meeting over his chest. He had a good hundred pounds on Stel, yet here she was dragging him backward by herself.

Knowing Stel, she had a damn good reason for killing the bastard. One I didn't want to know, otherwise I'd be digging him up just so I'd have the pleasure of plunging the knife into him myself.

Shaking those thoughts away, I kicked into action, grabbing his feet, and helping her dump his body behind the SUV where we'd just fucked. Stel shoved the bloody knife into my saddlebag and rushed to the side of the parking garage, looking down. She must be checking to see which way the town car was headed. Phone in hand, I dialed the only person I knew of who could take care of this shit for us.

Hunter picked up on the second ring and I didn't even give him a chance to speak.

"Hey, I need a cleanup at 4240 West Ross. Body's behind an SUV. Stel and I are going after the second guy."

Stel jogged over as I hung up and climbed

on behind me, her voice breathless as she said, "Take a right. He's heading out of town."

Her hands tightened around me as I took off, quickly navigating the sloping ramps downward.

We needed to catch up to the town car before we lost him. Thankfully, traffic was light, and I could weave in and out of the cars. Up ahead, I spotted his car and slowed down. If he was talking about Stel, and I strongly suspected that he was, he wasn't getting within a hundred yards of her.

The farther he drove, the more I had to fall back. Wide open fields and winding roads didn't provide much cover. When I rounded the last bend, I couldn't even see his taillights. Stel tapped me and pointed to the dirt road. Sure enough, there was dust still floating in the air.

We passed the dirt road and did a U-turn. From this angle, I could see the black bike sitting among a stand of trees set farther back off the dirt road. What in the fuck was Ryder doing way out here? 'Cause this sure didn't look like the shitty bar Los Sepultureros members usually hung out at.

Stel tensed behind me. Yeah, she felt it too. Something wasn't right. Maybe we oughta figure out what in the hell was going on here before we went wandering around. Parking my bike beside his, I pulled out my phone and shot him a text.

His response was almost immediate. Stay

put.

Stel swung her leg off the bike and as soon as her feet hit the grass, she began pacing. Me? Cigarettes were more my speed, and it had been a hell of a fucking afternoon. Stel raised an eyebrow but didn't comment as I lit up. The nicotine hit me like a jolt to the system and I sighed.

Ryder came into view, his long legs eating up the distance as he ran toward us. His chest heaved when he finally stopped in front of Stel, his dark eyes giving her a once over, something I very much took offense to. He'd guessed at my feelings for Stel when we were in high school, so why in the fuck would he think I'd ever let any harm come to her?

"What happened to lying low at Hunter's?"

Since he was looking to her for answers, and asking her nicely, I decided it was best to keep my mouth shut. For now. If he got any ideas about disrespecting Stel, though, he might just find himself lying in the grass instead of standing.

"Jules sent the CIA a list of Antonio's known associates, and a few of the names were unfamiliar. I wanted to see if I recognized any of the men from the list, so I asked Switch to come with me. The man we followed here was at the club the night I was taken and just met with one of my captors."

She crossed her arms over her chest. "Your

turn. What the fuck are you doing here?"

Ryder's nose wrinkled like he'd just stepped in dog shit. "Spying on Los Sepultureros."

Evidently, I'd missed out on more shit than I thought between licking my wounds and leaving town. But catching up would have to wait because we'd just stumbled on to our missing link.

CHAPTER 26

STELLA

When I saw the creep who'd tried to feel me up in the club on the night I was taken in that elevator, I almost couldn't believe it. But the real kicker was when I watched Michael, that angelic devil, getting out of his pretty boy sports car. Talk about the right place at the right time.

Michael's voice as he'd addressed his boss was like being thrown back into that first cell all over again and I had to swallow back the bile filling my throat. When I heard them say they'd been trying to find me, an icy shiver of dread slid down my spine. Over my dead body were either of those assholes ever laying a hand on me, or anyone in my family.

Michael's death had been entirely too swift, but feeling my blade sinking into his skin, having his blood coating my hands, had been cathartic. It had unlocked shackles I wasn't even aware I still wore. If I could have, I would have killed them both in that garage and not thought twice about it.

But Mr. Stephen Day was no underling. While that meant he had escaped his fate, for now, that sick fuck's days were numbered.

I was going to take my time with him too. Maybe give him a taste of his own medicine, throw him in a cage naked for a few days and see how he liked that shit. Though, knowing his tastes, he might actually get off on it. In which case, I'd settle for a painfully slow death.

Switch's thick thigh brushed against mine, jerking me out of my vengeful thoughts. He seemed to do that quite a lot. He made me forget all about my revenge. He and his dick came damn close to disrupting my plans today. If those men had shown up a few minutes earlier, we might not be at the clubhouse now, listening to grown men bicker.

They'd been sitting around the table for half an hour now, and by the sound of things they weren't any further ahead than when they'd started. Their constant yakking was giving me a headache. Maybe it was time to tell them of my plans, and then all they had to do was decide if they were going to help me or leave me to it.

The room descended into silence when I stood, multiple sets of eyes watching my progress as I walked to where Ryder sat at the head of the table.

I planted my palms on its polished surface and leaned forward. "I'm going to take their money, then I'm going to take their lives, with or without your help. Decide which it's going to be."

Tweak's dark eyes met mine, a twinkle in them. "Okay, killer. I'll bite. How do you propose we steal their money?"

He'd always had a mischievous side, and as long as my brand of justice wasn't being directed at him, Tweak was always happy to help. Nobody, Switch included, knew he'd had a hand in painting the pink flames on the side of Ryder's gas tank. Not that I thought bringing down a human trafficking ring was in the same hemisphere as petty vandalism.

"Easy. We hit their safe houses. With no women to sell, or a place to store any more new ones, they will have nothing. What took them years to build we can wipe out in a matter of days."

"How do you plan to handle retaliation?" Ryder asked, his hand knocking against the wood beside mine. "These men won't take you destroying their multibillion-dollar business lying down."

"Did you not hear the second part of her plan?" Beast ran a hand down his dark beard and sighed. "Dead men can't very well come after us, now can they."

Hunter tilted his head to the side, his light eyes settling on me. "Assuming none of the players take off for parts unknown."

Switch leaned forward in his chair off to the side, his legs sprawling wide, his hands dangling between them. I stared down at his fingers. Fingers that had dug into my ass while he pounded into me, making me come so hard that I saw stars. Fucking stars.

No. Bad Stella. Get your mind out of the gutter before he either distracted you again, or the guys figured out what you'd been doing in that garage with Switch.

I tore my eyes away from his hands only to face Hunter's unnerving stare. He pinned me there, stripping me down to the bone as if he were a human x-ray machine.

"There's too much money on the line for them to go very far."

Hunter's eyes shifted to Switch, and I let out a breath. Part of what made Hunter so lethal was that there was no freeing yourself from his hold until he'd gotten exactly what he wanted and let you go.

Hunter may have suspected something was up between me and Switch, but now he knew for sure. There was no way someone as adept at reading people as he is would have missed it. But Hunter never used information unless it somehow benefited him. Thankfully, I didn't see how it ever could.

"They will come out only after their underlings fail. If we do this, we do it knowing we need to wipe out all the pawns on the board before the king makes his move."

Hunter's ominous words left behind an unsettling silence. I hated like hell that I'd put them in this position, but like it or not, I couldn't change the past. All I could do now was try to move forward. I'd respect their decision, and not hold it against them no matter how they voted, but I meant what I said. I was taking these men down. Even if it killed me.

Gunner ran a hand through his shaggy locks, his haunted eyes meeting mine. The man had more hidden ghosts than *Ghostbusters*, and I respected the hell out of him for it. He thought himself a monster, but sometimes it took a monster to fight monsters. To me, that made him more of a hero than his service to our country.

"If they could take you, what's stopping them from coming after our old ladies? I made a promise to Trish when I joined this club that I'd protect her. By helping you, I'm keeping that promise. No matter what the club decides, you can count on my rifle to hit any target you point it at."

Well, shit. Tears threatened to gather at the back of my eyes. If I were the hugging sort, like Cherry, I'd have knocked him over with the force of it already.

Ryder banged his gavel against the table. "If nobody else has anything more to report on this matter, I say we vote."

My father nodded at him, "I think you already know which way I'm voting."

From beside him, Pops clapped him on the back, then slid his hand to his shoulder, letting it rest there. "You know I'm with you until the end, brother."

Dagger leaned forward to look past Pops at my dad. "Hell, if it weren't for you, I wouldn't even be here. Brothers until the end."

My dad wiped underneath his eye with his thumb as Gunner raised a finger in the air to solidify his vote.

"Hell yes!" Tweak grinned at me. "You know I'm always up for some mayhem."

Beast sat next to Tweak, shaking his head. "Someone needs to keep an eye on wonder boy over here and make sure he doesn't get his ass shot off. I'm in."

"I've been watching this Antonio guy and something about him doesn't sit right with me," Colt said with a frown. "That's a yes for me."

Valentina's brother, Marco, flashed his white teeth at me. I wouldn't call it a smile, necessarily, because there was something predatory about it.

Switch shifted slightly, his body tightening, but I doubt anyone besides Hunter and I noticed.

Switch's desire to inflict violence on a man for looking at me in a manner he didn't like should have pissed me off. This wasn't the 1920s, and I didn't need Switch to handle shit for me. I could put Marco in his place my damn self, thank you very much.

Still, I couldn't deny that Switch's aggression had me rubbing my thighs together to keep from riding him like a bull in front of everybody. What the hell was happening to me? My hormones were single-handedly setting women's lib back at least forty years.

"I like you." Marco pointed his finger at me, and I swear I could hear Switch's teeth grinding from here. "You are bloodthirsty, you have cojones the size of watermelons, and I think you're just loco enough to pull this off. Yes, I will help you get your revenge."

"You don't get a vote, prospect," Switch snapped, his hands balling into fists.

Holy shit. They needed to hurry up and vote before I did something I'd regret.

Ryder leaned back in his chair to give Switch a death glare. "Neither do you, so pipe down over there before I toss you out on your ass."

Switch wisely kept his mouth shut, but I suspected that was mainly because he didn't trust Marco. Not that I trusted him, either. Valentina was one thing, she'd already gone against her family for Ryder and the club, but I suspected Marco's loyalty, if he had any, was with their brother, Diego.

Marco had been born into the Mexican cartel like I'd been born into the MC. The only difference between us was that I was here by choice.

Ryder straightened in his chair and looked over at Hunter. "What's your vote?"

"Yes."

When he added nothing else, Ryder banged the gavel. "Then it's unanimous. We start tonight at ten, so everybody get some rest. Hunter, if any of the locations are grouped together, I'd like to hit those first. Let's show them what we think of them taking one of our own."

I stood next to Ryder, astounded, as all the men started banging on the table and grunting. Wait. They thought of me as one of their own?

CHAPTER 27

STELLA

This location was different from any of the ones they'd kept me at. For starters, it was a damn strip mall. Women came here to get their nails done, their hair cut, or for a massage every day not knowing what was happening on the other side of the wall. I wasn't sure whether I should be horrified or impressed.

Switch nodded to me before he shot the lock off the door connected to the hair salon and kicked it in. He twisted to the side as gunfire erupted, flattening himself against the wall on the other side of the door jamb. Across from him, I mimicked his pose, waiting for his signal.

When there was a break in the gunfire, he pointed at me and then down, and I nodded, letting him know I'd go low while he went high. Crouching down, I fired through the doorway while Switch stood above me doing the same. We both stopped when the only gunfire we heard was coming from our side.

Switch pushed me behind him, and I gave him a disgruntled huff but let him go in first. Not because he was a man, or because I was pandering to his macho desire to protect me, but because he was the better shot. I wasn't dumb enough to die for vanity's sake.

He was humble about his abilities, to the point he was almost secretive about them, but he was just as talented as Gunner. They were merely opposite sides of the same coin. Both could shoot any gun you gave them and hit the bull's-eye, but Gunner specialized more in long-range shooting whereas Switch was better with the up close and personal kill.

When I stepped from behind Switch, I stared down at a man I didn't recognize in black fatigues. His body was slumped over on the floor, covered in blood, a bullet hole in the center of his forehead. That sure as hell wasn't me. Not that I hadn't put a few holes in him. It looked like I'd hit him in the stomach and leg.

"Good riddance," I said, spitting on his corpse. Every last one of these fuckers was going to get what was coming to them.

A woman sniffled behind me, and I turned around. Only it wasn't a woman sitting in that cell, but a teenager. Jesus Christ.

"Were you hit?"

She blinked up at me from atop her cot, her knees drawn up to her chin. But she didn't answer me.

"Are you okay?"

Her lithe frame shook so hard it rocked the cot. Shit. Maybe she was in shock or something. I dropped to my haunches beside the dead guard and started searching his pants pockets. I found two sets of keys, but one was clearly for a car.

When I approached her cell, she shrank in on herself, and I tried not to make a bunch of noise as I unlocked her cell.

"Here," I said, tossing the keys to Switch. "Set the other girl free while I try to coax this one out."

A ghost of a smile teased his lips before he turned and walked over to the only other cell in the room.

I left the door wide open and stepped inside. These cells were like the ones I was used to, steel bars, a cot, toilet, sink, and not much else. The floors here were concrete as well, the surface cold and hard beneath my butt as I sat down beside her cot.

My head rested on my knees with my hands loosely joined around the middle of my legs.

"My name's Stella. What's yours?"

She sniffed and buried her head in her knees as she whispered, "Bree."

Her red hair fell in a heavy mass of curls at the middle of her back, spreading around her like a ring of fire.

"Well, Bree, these assholes had me locked up in a cell too."

She raised her head, her piercing green eyes carefully watching me. "They did?"

"Yup." I pointed to where Switch was handing the other girl his T-shirt to put on. Damn him and his muscular tattooed self. Where was I? Oh, yeah. "He and the rest of The Devil's Deviants rescued me. And you know what?"

Her eyes widened. "What?"

"I'm going to kill them all, so they can never bother nice girls like you ever again."

"Jesus Stel," Switch muttered from outside of the bars, the other girl huddled at his side. "You're going to give the poor girl nightmares."

I snorted. "Like she won't have them every time she shuts her eyes, anyway. At least this way she knows as long as I'm around they won't be coming back for her."

"Do you mean it?"

There was a tinge of excitement mixed with hope in her words and I pretended to scratch the side of my face while giving Switch the finger. He didn't know shit. For once, I said just the right thing.

His chuckle echoed around the small room before his boots shuffled toward the door. It was time to hand these girls off to the old timers so we could hit the next safe house.

"Cross my heart and hope to die." I unclasped my arms and leaned back so I could cross my heart with my finger. "Now, what do you say I give you my T-shirt and we get out of here? No offense, but your accommodations suck ass."

Her laugh was oddly surprising. It came out full and throaty like a woman's rather than the girlish giggle I was expecting. Maybe she was older than she looked?

"What are you going to wear, then?"

I stood, took off my T-shirt, and handed it to her. "I'll be fine in a bra and jeans. Trust me, it's nothing these boys haven't seen before."

And that was the god's honest truth. The she-devil's, a.k.a. club groupies, paraded around the clubhouse in far less. Plus, something told me Switch would either find me a shirt or I'd be wearing his cut before this night was out.

CHAPTER 28

SWITCH

Stel had looked sexy as fuck in nothing but a bra and my cut last night. That was why, exhausted or not, I had to fuck her until we both passed out. Hell, I think I fell asleep inside her, which was as close to heaven as a guy like me could ever hope to get.

Most of the time, I liked it when Stel fought me, but I was glad she hadn't last night. We both needed the comfort of holding each other tight. Stel would never admit it, but rescuing all those women had taken its toll on her emotionally, and I wasn't ashamed to admit I needed the reassurance.

She had to do this, for her, and I admired the fuck out of her for it. But her being in the line of fire wasn't something I was ever gonna get used to. That wasn't a macho, beat-my-chest reaction —though she brought those out in me too—but an understanding that I couldn't live without her.

My Stel was as wild as a mustang, but in sleep she looked like an angel. Her blond hair was fanned out over my arm, her heart-shaped face turned upward begging to be kissed. She had an arm flung across my waist and her legs were intertwined with mine. Watching her like this was peaceful, and I wished time could stand still.

But then her eyelashes fluttered, and her eyes narrowed as she looked down at the outline of my hard dick underneath the sheet nudging at her arm. It was her fault for looking so damn beautiful among the rays of the setting sun that filtered through the window.

"He ain't getting any smaller with you staring at him like that."

She walloped me in the chest, hard, and I sucked in air trying not to laugh. Maybe if I teased her, she wouldn't be so willing to kick me out of her bed or run away.

"Asshole. Does he ever get tired?"

"Not around you."

That was the god's honest truth. My dick had become damn near prepubescent over the last couple of weeks. I'd like to think he was making up for lost time. Same as me.

I traced the side of her face, enjoying the feel of her creamy skin, admiring the view. She didn't swat my hand away or get up, so I took that as a green light. My girl liked it rough and dirty, and I was not about to complain about that, but sometimes, like now, I wanted to be sweet with my words and my actions.

She wasn't ready for promises or pretty words. I knew that, not that I was a flowery speaker by any stretch. But I wanted to show her, without my dick for once—sorry buddy you'd have to wait for a few minutes—that I loved her, and I knew that she loved me. Even if she wasn't ready to admit it.

"You remember the day you showed up at my trailer and found my dad whaling on me in the front yard?"

"Yeah," she said tentatively, stiffening in my hold.

"You dropped your bike and ran across the yard, jumping on his back, and pounding your little fists for all you were worth. I've still never seen anything quite as beautiful as your wrath. Then my old man peeled you off him and threw you to the side like you were nothing. The only person who'd ever given a shit about me was nothing to him, same as me."

I stroked a hand along her jaw. "That was the first time I'd ever hit him back, and I probably never would have stopped if it hadn't been for you yelling my name. When I looked up, there you were, tears streaking your face, motioning for me to come on. Sirens blared in the distance as you told me to get the fuck on, and then you drove me back to the club. Do you remember what you said to your dad?"

She rubbed her head against the palm of my hand. "I told him I wouldn't ask for anything for my birthday so long as he helped you."

"Nobody had ever stuck their neck out like that for me before." I placed a chaste kiss on her forehead. "And if that's not love, then I don't know what is."

When I leaned back to look at her, she tried to lower her gaze, but I wouldn't let her. She deserved to know this next part, and I was going to look her in the eye when I told her.

"Later that night, after you fell asleep, your dad and Pops took me home."

Her eyes widened, and her lips parted. She didn't know this part of our story.

"My old man was drunk as usual on the couch. He didn't even spare a glance at the two bikers who walked in with me. He spouted off about how he was pressing charges and had plenty of witnesses to make them stick too. Said there was already a warrant out for my arrest, but before they carted me off, he was gonna teach me one last lesson."

She sucked in a shuddered breath, knowing

the next part couldn't be good. And she'd be right.

"He reached for the belt sitting beside him, but he didn't get the chance to stand because your dad shot him. Then he looked over at me and told me to go pack a bag and be quick about it. When I came back, bag in hand, he patted me on the shoulder and told me to go with Pops. That he'd take care of everything. I asked him why he'd do that for me, and he said it was because you'd never asked him for anything before."

Her eyes were shiny pennies, their golden depths filled with unshed moisture.

"You saved me back then, gave me this wonderful life, and I'm going to do the same for you. We're going to see this through until the end, and then I'm going to ask you to be my old lady. Until then, all you gotta do is let me love you the only way I know how."

My lips fused against hers, sealing in my words. They may have been ineloquent and bloody, but they were from the heart. I'd always come for her, even when she didn't think she needed saving.

Our kiss was unhurried, soft, and needy. Her body shifted to mold against mine, her heartbeat finding the same rhythm as mine. They say there's a difference between fucking and making love and I figured it was about time to see if there was something to that myth.

So, I set about loving her with not only my heart but with my body as well. My lips trailed to the sensitive column of her throat, kissing and licking my way down to her collarbone. She shivered in my arms, little moans escaping her when I sucked her nipple into my mouth. Her skin was honey, the taste addictive and sweet.

Her little nails bit into the back of my head as she pulled me closer, but I didn't let her hurry the pace any. The little disappointed mewls that came from her were adorable as fuck as I kissed my way to her other nipple. No matter how long I lived I'd never get tired of paying homage to the most glorious set of tits I'd ever seen.

She shifted beneath me, rubbing herself against me, trying to entice me to fuck her. This girl was going to be the death of me. But my dick could wait a little longer. I wanted to know how she tasted.

My tongue left a wet trail on her skin behind as I worked my way down until I was face to face with the prettiest pink pussy I'd ever seen. My mouth literally watered at the sight of her wet cunt.

"Get up here and fuck me."

This girl and her impatience.

"Not yet."

"Quit staring at my pussy."

"I'm gonna look at your pretty little cunt for as long as I damn well please. Then I'm going to eat your pussy until you come all over my face and I don't want to hear shit about it."

She stared down at me, biting her bottom lip, a pink flush on her cheeks. Fuck, was she self-conscious? If that was what the problem was, I'd end that shit real quick.

Holding her eyes, I swirled my tongue around her clit, watching her reaction. Her eyelashes fluttered and her tits jiggled from the force of her breathing. It was all over for her after that. I couldn't hold back even if I wanted to. I devoured her delicious cunt.

Her legs clamped down on either side of my head as I ate her out until I almost couldn't breathe, but what a way to go. There was no way I was stopping, not until her juices were flowing down my beard.

Stel's body tensed, and she screamed my name. It was fucking music to my ears. Her arousal was as sweet as the rest of her and as addicting. If my dick wasn't leaking everywhere, begging to be inside her, I'd lick her pussy for days.

Her body shivered as I slid upward, lifting her leg as I went. By the time our lips met, her ankle was by my ear and my cock was balls deep in her sweet pussy. The thought of her tasting her own arousal on my lips nearly drove me insane.

She grabbed my ass, her nails sinking in, pushing me farther into her with each thrust. Fuck me. This girl was going to be the death of me. She was sex personified, her every moan like audio porno. The last shred of my patience snapped, and I fucked her into the mattress. I wanted to own her as thoroughly as she owned me.

Another scream tore from her lips as she came around me and I was like an animal possessed. I couldn't get enough. It would never be enough. No matter how many times we made love, or fucked, or whatever you wanted to call it, it would never be enough.

"Tell me you're mine," I panted. "Tell me who owns this pretty cunt."

One hand caressed the side of my face while her other one pulled me more deeply inside her. "You. It's always been you."

My heart soared at her words, my body rushing to follow my heart. As I spilled into her, I buried my head in her neck, marking her as mine.

From the other side of the door came the bang of a fist, and then Hunter's bored voice. "Quit fucking and get out here. There's something you need to hear."

"Coming," Stel called out, already shoving at my chest.

Fuck me, couldn't a man enjoy his well-deserved orgasm around here? Stel shoved at me again. Guess not.

I rolled off her and lay on my back watching her scramble to find her clothes, her hair a mess, her body bearing the evidence of my marks.

"Are you just going to lie in bed watching while I get dressed," she huffed as she tugged on a pair of jeans—sans panties.

"Damn, you're beautiful."

It was true. Even annoyed, first thing in the morning, looking thoroughly fucked thanks to yours truly, she was stunning. So much so that sometimes it took my breath away.

"Yeah, well," she muttered, looking a bit flushed. "You still have to get your ass in gear."

She'd kill me for even thinking it, but she was fucking adorable right now. But she had a point. With a sigh, I dragged myself out of bed and started hunting for my jeans. Since I'd given away my T-shirt, I'd have to settle for throwing on my cut until we learned what the fuck had Hunter's boxers in a bunch.

Stel went straight over to Hunter's fancy coffee maker, trying to fix her hair as she went. Brandy sat at the long wooden table in the kitchen, her face pale. Shit.

Her eyes met mine, the gold flecks in them reminding me of Stel, only her irises were greener. Funny how I'd never noticed they both had hazel eyes before now.

"Colt called me and asked if I could hack into the security feed at Antonio's club and listen in on a conversation. He said a man had stormed into Antonio's club about a half hour ago, and Antonio told him to shut his mouth, then quickly ushered him into his office and shut the door. Colt didn't dare try to listen at the door because the club won't open for another couple of hours, and he'd have no way of explaining what he was doing there if he got caught."

Stel sat down beside her, her arms around a mug blowing on the steam.

Brandy turned to her friend. "I'm going to warn you before I start playing the recording that it's going to be difficult for you to hear."

"Thanks for the heads up." Stel nodded at Brandy's laptop sitting on the table. "But go ahead, I can handle it."

Brandy hit a button, and I started at the slam of a door.

"You know better than to come here before the club opens," a man hissed.

"Would you like me to come back later for your share of the one point two million we owe?"

I recognized the voice of the second man. It was the creep from the parking garage that we followed out to where Ryder was spying on Los Sepultureros. The same one that Stel said was at the club meeting with Antonio the night she was taken.

"What are you talking about?"

"Well, when you have customers who have already paid for girls, and those girls are now gone, they're going to want their money back. Have time to see me now, Antonio?"

"Gone, what do you mean the girls are gone?

They're sitting naked in cells, for fuck's sake."

"Someone set fire to three of our safe houses last night, and my men tell me there were only about a dozen charred remains. That means whoever did this took the women."

"Fuck," Antonio screamed.

"And I'm willing to bet it was your little pet, no doubt with the help of her father's club. I told you when she escaped that she was going to be a problem."

"A problem I tasked you with taking care of."

Antonio was a dead man. He just didn't know it yet.

"Don't put this on me. The agent was a problem for both of us, and he's been taken care of, but the girl was all you."

"You act like you don't have your own troubles with women. At least I didn't accidentally try to sell the sister of a CIA agent. How is the search going, by the way?"

Speaking of Delilah, where the fuck was she? My head turned in a swivel, looking for her when Hunter caught my eye. He mouthed 'bedroom' and pointed down the hall. Fuck. She must have heard the recording first and needed a minute.

"That's rich coming from the man who made that same agent his first lieutenant."

"Fine, we both fucked up. Happy now?" A chair creaked in the background. "We thought we had all our problems taken care of only to wind up with two missing girls who can fuck us and a damn motorcycle club breathing down our necks. Now, can we maybe discuss how we're going to fucking fix this before we either get killed or go broke?"

"It's not a secret that Los Sepultureros and The Devil's Deviants are rivals. We could always make it look like a turf war. You supply Los Sepultureros with the weapons, and I'll take care of making sure The Deviants know they were the ones who took Stella. Then we sit back and let them kill each other."

"I like it. The Deviants will be too busy fighting the wrong men to keep fucking with our business and Stella's stupid enough to involve herself in her father's war. That only leaves the sister. What do you want to do about her?"

"Mateo hooked her the first time, maybe we can send Michael after her this time? He can charm the panties off any woman."

"Fine, but tell him there can be no screw ups this time. Now, get out of my club before someone recognizes you."

The recording stopped, and I looked over at Stel. She stared off into space, a blank look on her face. After all that, I suspected a much stronger reaction from her.

"Stel?"

My tone was soft, but she still jumped. She blinked a few times, her honey eyes meeting mine.

"What?"

"Are you okay?"

"Yeah," she said, setting her coffee mug down and standing. "I'm just going to go take a shower and check on Delilah."

I watched her walk down the hall, dread settling in the pit of my stomach. She was turning something over inside that brain of hers, and I got the feeling I wasn't going to like it. Not one bit.

CHAPTER 29

STELLA

The club had no choice now but to go after Antonio. He was planning to arm our rivals and start a war. But I wasn't letting anyone kill that asshole but me. If he thought he could get rid of me that easily, he had another thing coming. He didn't know who he was messing with, but he was about to find out. All I had to do was get to him before the club did.

Which meant I had to sneak out without anyone noticing, a nearly impossible feat with Switch wanting to fuck me twenty-four seven. Not that my pussy minded. No, that traitorous bitch was like that creepy dude from *Lord of the Rings* stroking that ring. My precious. Fucking pitiful was what it was.

I slipped into Delilah's room, not bothering to knock. She sat on the bed with her legs crossed, staring off into space. That recording had fucked with her like it had fucked with me, but for different reasons.

While she had closure, and now knew she had nothing to do with her brother's death, it still wouldn't bring him back. Nothing would.

But I could kill the man responsible for his death. All I needed her to do was distract Switch.

She didn't look up or even blink when I approached the bed, so I snapped my fingers in front of her face. I hated disturbing her sorrow like that, but justice waited for no man. At least, not today, it didn't.

Her dark eyes focused on me, then she turned her head away. "Leave me alone."

"I wish I could, but I only have a brief window to kill the man responsible for your brother's death."

Her head turned back to me so fast I was surprised it didn't give her whiplash. Yeah, I'd say I had her attention.

"All you have to do is keep Switch busy with training for as long as you can. I'll do the rest."

"Deal." She held out her hand, then snatched it away before I could take it. "But when it comes time to kill Mateo, you leave him to me."

She put her hand out again, and I smiled down at her as I shook it. "Pleasure doing business with you. Now, if you'll excuse me, I'm off to fake a shower."

Her laugh followed me out the door, but like everything else about her, it lacked any sort of feeling. I only hoped when this was all over that she found the will to shuck the empty shell and live again. If not for herself, then for Jules because he would never get the chance.

In my room, I went straight to the bedside table and slid open the drawer. The gun my dad had given me for my sixteenth birthday sat in the bottom. He gave it to Hunter the second night I was here thinking it would somehow make me feel safe. If only that were true.

When we left to hit the safe houses, Switch had handed me one of his. I took it and never corrected his assumption. What made me keep it a secret from him I couldn't tell you, but now I was glad that I had.

I turned the shower nozzle to hot, letting steam fill the room before I stood on the toilet and opened the window. Peeking out, I watched Delilah lead Switch away from the house with a determined look on her face.

Now was my chance. It was a tight fit, and took some *Cirque Du Soleil* maneuvering, but at least I landed in the grass. I brushed off my jeans and looked around, but Delilah and Switch were far enough away that they hadn't heard me fall.

Keeping low to the ground, I made a break for Brandy's SUV with the key I'd stolen from the bowl on the front table before I went to Delilah's room. When it came to forgiveness, I could only hope that Brandy was like her sister. Valentina stole Cherry's car once and drove it all the way to Mexico, and Cherry forgave her. At least I was only taking Brandy's car across town and bringing it right back.

On the way to Antonio's club, I kept looking in my rearview mirror, expecting to see a man on a chrome machine bearing down on me. But that never happened, and I let out a relieved breath as I pulled around back and killed the engine.

The sun had set on my ride in, and as I stepped out into the darkness of the parking lot, I halfway expected to be accosted by one of Antonio's goons. While the lot was filled with cars, nobody seemed to be around. Probably because they were all busy getting the club ready to open.

Gingerly, I opened one of the heavy metal doors at the back of the club and poked my head in. This part of the club housed cases of liquor, wine, and beer to make unloading easier. There was nobody back here at the moment, so I snuck in, softly shutting the door behind me.

From the doorway, I could hear voices farther down the hall, but if I hurried, I could make it to the ladies' room and slip inside. Quickly, I closed the door behind me and pressed my ear against it. After the voices moved past the door, I waited a few seconds, and swung the door open, making my way down the hall.

This next part would be the hardest. The stairs. You could see everyone going up and down them, or at least their legs. All the staff wore black pants, and I had on jeans. There was nothing I could do about it now, so I'd just have to hurry up and hope nobody stopped me.

Halfway up to the third floor my luck ran out.

One of the bartenders from the private floor above smiled down at me. He was around my age, knew my favorite brand of beer, and collected muscle cars. That instantly made him my favorite. Damn. I hoped I didn't have to shoot him and stuff him in a closet or something.

"Long time no see. Where have you been, girl?"

Trapped in a cage naked thanks to your boss. Get that new cylinder for the sixty-eight *Mustang* yet? Yeah right. While I'd love to see the look on his face, I doubted honesty would get me very far.

"Just been busy over at the shop. Work piling up. You know how it is."

The part about work piling up was probably true. With only Tweak there to hold down the fort, I could only imagine the mess he'd made of my beloved shop. I bet none of my tools were in the right place.

"Yeah, I've been too busy working to finish the Stang."

"Damn shame." I pointed upstairs. "Better get going, Antonio is expecting me."

He got this funny look on his face, and I reached behind me for the gun I had tucked away in my waistband. Right when my hand closed around it, he spoke.

"He's in his office."

Dropping my hand, I said, "Thanks," and ran up the remaining steps.

Antonio's office was down the hallway, just off the stairs, so it didn't take me long to find him. His door opened with a crash, the girl that was bouncing on his dick falling backward onto the floor, narrowly missing the coffee table. This fucker.

I pointed the gun at her, then used it to motion to the door as I walked into the room. "Out. Now."

She grabbed her clothes and shoes off the floor, not bothering to get dressed, hurried past me, and closed the door on her way out. Wise girl.

Antonio sat there smiling with his wet dick still hanging out of his pants. His hands were spread out on the back of the black leather couch like he didn't have a care in the world. He probably thought I was bluffing before when I told him I knew how to shoot.

"Stella," he purred my name, and I wanted

to cringe. Why had I ever thought fucking him was a good idea? "So nice to see you alive and well. When you disappeared without a trace, I thought my enemies had gotten to you despite my best efforts."

"Save it," I hissed. "I know you're the one behind my descent into hell."

His face transformed. Gone was the suave businessman and in his place sat the devil.

"You've been spying on me since breaking free, haven't you?"

"You really should be more careful of the company you keep."

"So, it would seem. Then you know Mateo, no?"

This was some kind of test. But why? I was the one holding a gun while he sat there with his fly open.

"We became acquainted when he shot Jules in front of me and then left his corpse to rot with me in a cell."

He lifted his hand off the sofa, but when I took a step forward, he set it back down.

"Yes, well, I'm afraid my friends, Los Sepultureros, are a little overzealous in their hatred. You understand. No?"

He watched me carefully, waiting to see my reaction. Interesting. Antonio wasn't sure if I knew who Mateo was. Unfortunately for him, I had an excellent poker face.

"Interesting choice of friends given you were

fucking the daughter of their rival don't you think?"

"Our association is regrettable." A note of annoyance crept into his carefully orchestrated neutral tone. "They can't even do a drive by without screwing it up. Then I do Marco a favor and hand him his revenge on a silver platter and what does he do? Let you get away. No wonder The Deviants have always come out on top."

The sound of a gunshot rang out in his small office, a string of curses leaving his lips as his arms fell from the back of the couch. He pressed a hand to his thigh where red was taking over the gray of his dress pants, hatred burning in his gaze.

His teeth clenched, he bit out, "You fucking shot me."

"Felt fantastic, too. I wish I could stay longer and torture you, but I'm afraid your little girlfriend might tattle on me. So, I really must kill you now and be on my way."

He threw his head back and laughed. Well, that wasn't the reaction I was hoping for. You'd think he'd at least be apprehensive. Maybe I needed to be scarier. So, I shot him in the chest this time.

His laughter died as I cocked my gun and took aim, this time at his head.

One minute he was sitting on the couch, and in the next he was reaching underneath the coffee table, a glint of silver catching my eye as he raised his hand.

It was then I realized my mistake. When I no longer had the element of surprise on my side, I'd lost the upper hand. Antonio had been toying with me the whole time. He wanted me to know all the ways he'd fucked me over before he pulled the trigger. Before he ended things for good.

He fired, the sound of his gunshot ringing in my ears, my breath leaving me in a rush as I was tackled to the ground. A heavy weight blanketed me, pressing me into the floor, pain radiating out from my hipbone.

I turned my head to find a pair of cinnamon eyes glaring down at me. His mouth was a flat hard line and his nostrils flared. The look on his face promised pain and punishment, and my body responded. Only, it wasn't fear that I felt.

"I'm going to tell you how this is going to go. You're going to take the bullet out of my shoulder, drop to your knees, and choke on my cock. After I've finished coming down your pretty little throat, I'm going to flip you over, tan your ass red, and then fuck you into the mattress while you scream that you'll never pull a stunt like this again. You feel me?"

CHAPTER 30

SWITCH

When Pops told me Stel took Brandy's car, I knew exactly where she was headed. Luckily, I arrived just in time. Antonio had his gun pointed at my reason for living.

Our bullets left the chamber at the same time, and I dove for Stel, turning myself into a human shield. If I had to do it all over again, I'd take the bullet that was meant for her. Every damn time.

That didn't mean she was off the hook. Far from it. I meant what I told her on the floor of Antonio's office. She would pay for this little stunt of hers. She needed to understand that she was living not only for herself, but for me as well.

Hunter had given me some pills that made my pain manageable after Stel finished stitching me up. Her technique could damn near rival that of an ER nurse by this point, so I knew my wound would heal, leaving behind only a faint line where the bullet had entered.

Stel's mom never had the stomach for patching Mad Dog up, so Stel had taken over that job at the tender age of eight. Pretty soon she was sewing up Pops, Dagger, and anyone else who needed it. She never was one to shy away from anything, be it bullets, blood, guns, or even making up for my shoulder wound.

My hand threaded through her blond hair, setting the pace as her head bobbed up and down. Her honey eyes were glued to my face, watching my every reaction. She was the sexiest thing I'd ever seen, sprawled between my legs, her round, peach-shaped ass in the air.

Lord have mercy. The sight before me almost made it worth getting shot. Almost. But not quite. There was still the matter of her punishment, but first, we needed to get something straight.

The pout on her lips as I pulled her off my cock made my lips pull up into a smirk. "Lie across my stomach, ass up, ready to receive your punishment."

She raised a blond brow but complied. I took a moment to stare at her ass, 'cause damn, before I spoke again.

"Repeat after me."

She turned her head, her long hair falling over her shoulder.

"I will never again be careless with my life."

Smack.

She sucked in a breath through her teeth and repeated my words.

"Because I'm responsible for two lives now."

Smack. The sound reverberated around the room, a red handprint, my handprint, on each ass cheek.

Her eyes widened. "I…I don't understand."

Smack. "Repeat what I said."

This time she complied, adding a hissed fuck before the words.

"There is no Switch without Stella."

Smack.

She stared back at her red ass cheeks as she repeated my words.

"If I die, then so will he."

Smack.

Her honey eyes darted from her ass to my face as she shook her head no.

Smack.

"You can say no all you want, but it won't make my words any less true. I will always come for you. Now repeat what I said."

Smack.

She was still shaking her head no, the trace of a tear at the corner of her eye, but she carefully repeated my words.

My hands massaged away the sting I'd just inflicted, a little moan escaping her as she watched me over her shoulder. Her ass lifted underneath my hand as she went back on her haunches.

My eyes trailed down her side, coming to rest on the profile of her breast, her nipple erect and begging for my mouth. She shifted her weight, swinging one leg over my lap, straddling me. Her hands cradled my face, drawing my eyes back up to meet hers. Fuck, she was beautiful.

"I will honor those words on two conditions."

"I'm listening."

"They must also apply to you. No more jumping in front of bullets."

"I won't if you won't," I challenged. "What's the second condition?"

She smiled her coy half smile, the one she reserved for only me. "If you so much as look at another woman I'll cut your balls off and hang them like a goddamned pair of fuzzy dice from the handlebars of my bike. You feel me?"

"You don't have to worry about that," I said, a smile tugging at my lips as I stared up at her. "The only pussy I'm gonna chase is mine. Now, are you going to give me my pussy, or do I need to take it?"

"Take it." Her eyebrow rose. "If you can."

Shit. She should know by now there was nothing I loved more than a challenge.

Her mouth formed a perfect O as I grabbed her hips and flipped her onto her stomach on the mattress. She bucked against me and moaned as I lifted her ass into the air with one hand while using the other to trap her beneath me.

"Now, be a good girl and scream my name every time my cock bottoms out in that pretty little pussy of yours."

Her head was turned to the side, her hair half covering her face. "I thought it was supposed to be your pussy. My bad."

This fucking girl and her mouth. She was going to choke on those words as she took my cock.

She inhaled sharply as I entered her in one swift go. Her ass bore my handprint, and I ran the rough pads of my fingers over the mark and up her back as I slid almost all the way out. My hand tangled in her soft blond strands, tugging her head back as I thrust back inside her wet pussy. Excuse me, *my* wet pussy, because there was no mistaking that I owned that shit.

Her breathing became erratic as she clamped down on my cock. Fuck, she was close, and I needed her to come like I needed air. Picking up the pace, I pounded into her, watching her lips part on the scream I'd asked her for.

She drew out my name like it had twenty

syllables instead of one.

I tugged on her hair until my mouth reached her ear. "I don't think I heard you right the first time. Whose pussy was it?"

"Fucker."

"Try again," I taunted as I pounded into her, her pussy damn near strangling me.

"Switch's p...p...fuckkk!"

Her pussy spasmed around me with the force of her orgasm and I followed her over the edge spilling into her. Both our chests heaved, our breaths in sync, a bead of sweat trickling down the delicate line of her neck. My tongue darted out to lap it up, her skin warm and sweet against my tongue.

She moaned, the contented sound reaching deep inside my chest, warming it. And she thought I could ever want anyone else. There was no going back to scraps after you'd dined on prime rib.

"We have to get ready."

Stel didn't sound the slightest bit happy about it either, which surprised me. With Antonio out of the picture, the club decided to eliminate Los Sepultureros before we went after any more safe houses. Which meant Stel would get her shot at killing Mateo.

This wouldn't be the first time I'd had to fight injured, so I knew from personal experience that tonight was going to suck. The wound was high enough on my shoulder that it wouldn't affect my aim, but firing a gun, or a street brawl if it came to that, was still going to hurt like a bitch. Stel's reluctance, though, didn't make any sense to me.

"The club can do without us tonight if you'd rather sit this one out."

"It's not that." She huffed, slipping from my grasp to turn and face me. "I'm worried about Delilah. She thinks she's ready to take on Mateo, but what if she isn't? What if he hurts her?"

My girl had a heart that was twice as big as her mouth. It was one of the many things I loved about her, so I didn't have the heart to tell her that I didn't think Delilah cared much if she made it out alive or not so long as Mateo went to his grave.

"Stel, she's going to go after him no matter what you say. All we can do is try our best to protect her while she does."

"I hate that you're right."

She was pouty, and lord knows I wanted to fuck that pout right off her face, but we had places to be. So, I gave Stel the next best thing to an orgasm.

"If you stick close to me, I think it'll be safe enough now that Antonio's dead for you to ride your bike tonight. What do you say I ask Hunter if we can ride out from the club rather than everybody meeting here?"

Stel threw her arms around my neck and gave me a kiss that damn near curled my toes. If my shoulder didn't hurt too bad later, maybe I'd say to hell with the new paint job and fuck her against her bike.

Then my night went to shit, all plans of fucking Stel forgotten.

CHAPTER 31

SWITCH

Delilah sat behind me on my bike while Stel rode on her baby beside me. I missed having Stel ride with me, but hearing her whoop of joy was a hell of a consolation prize. Plus, it was nice to see her looking more like her old self.

She didn't think I'd noticed the changes in her since Hunter pulled her from that warehouse, but I had. Stel had always known exactly who she was, and that gave her a quiet sort of confidence. One that had been noticeably absent as of late.

Not to mention the nightmares. They still

plagued her, but I'd chosen to kiss her awake when they did and pretend that I did it solely to screw her. She could keep her pride and I could avoid that tight feeling in my chest every time she chanted the word no in her sleep like it was a damn prayer.

For tonight, I'd watch her ride and ignore the tweak in my shoulder, pretending that everything was the way it used to be. Only, maybe better, because I never got to hold the old Stel in my arms at night.

Everyone in front of me slowed, instantly alert now that we were approaching the last turn before the dirt road that led to Los Sepultureros' hideout. We would have to kill our engines and walk the bikes from here on up to the stand of trees where I'd seen Ryder's bike last time.

Delilah hopped off my bike and walked over to Stel, helping her push her baby to the only hiding spot available to us. Once everyone's bike was under the trees, Gunner grabbed the canvas bag he kept his sniper rifle in and handed it to Valentina. Hell, what was happening right now? That man didn't let anyone touch that bag.

In usual form, she wore heels that sank into the grass, totally useless in my opinion, but even with the bag she easily kept pace with the rest of the guys.

The dark was our friend, and Ryder seemed to know the way. Still, we had to run between the groupings of trees that seemed to crop up out of nowhere.

An old farmhouse appeared out of the gloom, its porch lights like a beacon in the night. Ryder stopped and dropped to his haunches, the rest of us following his lead.

Valentina dropped the bag, Gunner right there to shine a flashlight on it. Well, I'll be damned. The girl started piecing together a sniper rifle.

It seemed everyone else was as transfixed as I was, standing around watching while her nimble fingers worked. After she was done, she handed it up to Gunner and got to work on the other one. Gunner must now carry two in his bag. Wasn't that something? Valentina and Gunner had his and hers sniper rifles. I bet Ryder just loved that shit.

Gunner turned his light off, casting us once again into darkness. Once my eyes adjusted, I could make out one of her heels on the ground. The two of them must work as a sniper team because we were now missing a shadow.

Hell, she might have even been the one to lay down cover fire at the warehouse for me to get inside. The rest of the men sure seemed to trust her looking down the scope of a sniper rifle, but the jury was still out for me. Not that I expected her to trust me any more than I trusted her. To her, I was probably just the asshole who left everyone high and dry.

Ryder's hushed whisper came from beside

Valentina. "We're going to split up into teams of two or three and surround the house. Take out any men you find outside quietly so we can make it inside the house without a problem."

Shadows started moving away, and I hissed, "Delilah and Stel, you're with me."

There was no way I'd let anyone else watch my girl's back, and I knew Delilah would stay glued to Stel until we found Mateo. If he was even here. I wasn't foolish enough to think we'd be able to kill them all, but after tonight they would no longer pose an immediate threat to Stel or the club.

Stel's vanilla scent teased my nostrils a second before I felt her heat at my back. Her presence calmed me almost as much as a cigarette as I moved away from Valentina. Being that Delilah still wasn't much of a fighter, and only a marginal shot, it would be best if I could keep her out of the fray as much as possible.

If I went around to the front and let the boys take point, then we could slip in the door behind them and search for Mateo. The sooner we got him, the better. Delilah might only be a shell of her former self, but she'd become determined to have her vengeance at any cost. And while I understood where she was coming from, I refused to let her drag Stel to the grave with her.

A few men with automatic weapons in their hands stood next to the front porch smoking. I motioned to the girls to stop. We'd wait here, a safe distance away, and let the guys take care of them.

The screen door swung open, and a man stepped onto the porch. He hissed something at the other two in Spanish, and they walked around back. Once they were out of sight, he raised a phone to his ear. He switched to English, but we were far enough away that I could only catch a few words.

As he spoke, he stepped beneath the porch light. The shaft of light illuminated his features, and I recognized him from the photo on Stel's laptop. I looked over at Delilah in time to see the shadow of the gun she held in her hand.

Placing my hand over the top of hers, I whispered, "Wait. You'll never be able to hit him from here and we'll lose the element of surprise."

She didn't move, or give any sign that she'd heard me, so I pressed my hand down on hers, forcing her hand back to her side.

Stel whispered, "Your time will come," as Mateo hung up and went back inside the house. To be on the safe side, I kept my hand over Delilah's.

The outlines of men moving low and close to the house were now visible, and I knew the cavalry had worked their way around to the front. And not a moment too soon. If I hadn't stopped Delilah, she would have alerted them to our presence. With that warning, and enough ammo, they might have been able to fend us off.

Carefully avoiding the porch light, one of the guys went for the screen door, opening it wide and waiting a second before they waved. Shadows started filing into the house, one by one, and I motioned for the girls to follow me across the lawn. We ran, single file, Stel's scent reassuring me she was on my heels.

When we reached the porch, the same guy still stood by the railing, holding the screen door open for us. As I looked up at him, the porch light cast a shadowy outline of spiky hair. We rushed the rest of the way up the steps, and slipped past Colt, the screen door softly clicking closed behind us.

There was no movement inside the dimly lit foyer or on the stairs. From deeper within the first floor of the house, I heard a TV blaring and then male laughter. Above us, a man walked along the landing and we waited for him to disappear behind the wall before we moved.

Beside the first doorway, we flattened ourselves against the wall. When I peeked around the corner, there was nothing but crates stacked half haphazardly all over the room.

The TV's volume became almost deafening as we moved past an empty bathroom that looked and smelled like it hadn't been cleaned in a few years. Jesus, what the hell did these guys eat?

Light from a TV poured out of the next room, and I stood beside the doorway listening. There didn't appear to be any movement or laughter coming from inside, so I chanced a look. A man that was almost as wide as he was tall sat in a recliner, the flickering light casting garish shadows over the blood pouring from his neck onto his white shirt. The guys must have already cleared this room.

Farther down the hallway I heard the crack of a pool cue hitting balls. The doorway was wide and based on the marks on the doorjamb there had been a door here at one point. Men laughed inside the room and then someone set a gaming controller or remote down on a table.

A man coughed three times, and then the room grew quiet. That couldn't be good. Fuck. I looked back at Stel, and she nodded, gun in hand. Colt moved up to block Delilah and nodded that he was also ready.

Something hit the floor, and by the sound of the thud, it was heavy. I snuck a quick glance around the corner, taking stock of the Mexican standoff happening on the other side of the wall. The situation wasn't pretty, but it wasn't anything Colt, Stel, and I couldn't handle.

"Hunter can't risk killing any more of their men because there are two guns being pointed at Ryder. I need you guys"—I looked between Stel and Colt—"to cover me so I can save Ryder's ass." My gaze swung to Delilah as I whisper hissed, "Mateo isn't in there, so I need you stay put and keep your head down until one of us comes back for you."

She shook her head and then slid down to the floor, covering her head with her hands.

I whispered, "One, two, three," then made my move.

Not surprisingly, Hunter was the first to notice me. That crazy fucker had his knife to the throat of a man almost twice his size, his light eyes watching as I moved behind the green couch. It looked like they stole the damn thing from their great grandma. Hopefully, she wouldn't be pissed about a few bullet holes.

"Ryder, down," I yelled as I fired the first shot, hoping he listened to me. If not, we might wind up with matching shoulder wounds.

The entire room had heeded my warning, well, except for Hunter, so my second shot wound up hitting the man in the middle of his chest. Shit. While everyone was still down, and slightly confused, I fired again, this time silencing the man rolling around on the ground beside Ryder.

A man roared as he stood, leveling his gun at me, but Hunter got to him before I could even fire. From behind me, I heard Delilah's startled cry. Which meant so did Stel. Fuck. Sorry guys, you'd just have to handle shit from here without me.

Using the couch as cover, I hunched down, searching the room for Stel. I found her over by the pool table, shooting over the top of it, inching her way closer to the doorway. There was a lot of open room between the pool table and the doorway, so she'd have to run for it.

When she sprang into action, I laid down cover fire until she made it through the doorway, then followed her, shooting behind me as I ran.

Out in the hallway, I saw a flash of Stel's blond ponytail as she ran out the front door. Mateo must be planning to use Delilah as a human shield so he could escape. Little did he know we had reinforcements outside. We just had to give them a clear shot because Gunner would never risk hitting Delilah, even if it meant letting Mateo go.

Using the shrubs that surrounded the house to camouflage my presence, I watched as Stel yelled Mateo's name. He stopped dragging Delilah across the lawn and turned, pulling her by the hair until she was flush against his body.

"Stella," he purred her name like a caress. Oh, yeah, this fucker wasn't leaving here alive. "I knew you were going to be a challenge, but I must admit, you've far surpassed my expectations."

Delilah didn't struggle in his hold, or even move. But her voice was clear and sure as she told Stel, "Kill him for me."

Stel had her gun trained on him, but I knew she'd never listen to Delilah. Even if Delilah didn't care if she died, Stel did.

"She won't risk killing her protégé, love," he

hissed. "What do you think, Stella? Can I still get at least fifty thousand for her?"

He was trying to goad Stel into shooting. He probably figured she'd kill Delilah and then he'd kill her. There was only one thing for me to do, and I hoped like hell Stel would forgive me for it.

I fired, watching as Delilah's body jerked. She could no longer hold herself upright and slumped in Mateo's arms, becoming dead weight.

"No," Stel screamed, falling to her knees on the ground.

A second shot rang out in the darkness and Mateo dropped to the ground, landing on top of Delilah. It wasn't the justice Delilah had envisioned, but she'd gotten what she wanted. Mateo was dead.

CHAPTER 32

STELLA

Delilah's dark eyes followed my jerky movements as I unraveled the gauze covering her thigh.

"You look pretty pissed for a girl who insists she's not."

Her assessment was fair, which only pissed me off even more.

"I'm fine," I huffed, pasting on a fake smile. "See."

"Why do you care so much if I live or die, anyway?"

That was a good question. Why did I care?

She started out as nothing more than a guilty obligation. If I could do right by her, then Jules wouldn't have died in vain. His death might not have been my fault, or by my hand, but the nagging guilt had stayed with me, anyway.

Was it because I'd given him so much shit in life? Was it because I felt like a shitty person for hating him while I talked to his corpse to stay sane? Or was it because I'd always wonder if I hadn't opened my big mouth if he'd have made it until the boys came?

Fuck if I knew. No matter what the reason, Jules's death had changed me. The vengeance I sought wasn't just for me. It was for all those who'd been taken and sold. And yes, when it came to his sister, I was a stage five clinger. So what? There were worse things I could be doing with my time than saving women. Even the ones who didn't want to be saved.

But she didn't need to know all that, especially the part about me talking to her brother's corpse.

"Because if you die, then the bad guys win, and nothing pisses me the fuck off more than that."

It might not have been pretty or elegant, but then again, neither was I. My mom always said people didn't know how to take me because I was honest and raw in a world of polished gems. And I figured she ought to know. There never lived a more polished or proper old lady than my mother.

Her brow furrowed. "I can't decide if you're smart or crazier than me."

The funny thing was, at this moment I couldn't either. When I stepped out of her room, I was going to war with a powerful man who stood to lose everything. The safer option would be to kill him and then set all the girls free, but somehow, I just couldn't do it. Death was too easy for a man like him.

He didn't give a shit how many lives he destroyed as long as he could afford his yacht in the Keys. So, I needed to take away the one thing he coveted more than anything else. Money. He needed to feel it all slipping away, the fancy apartment, cars, and expensive dinners out. Only then, when he had nothing left, would death come for him.

So, yes, I was crazy to take on a man like him when I didn't really have to. But I was smart enough to recruit help. Brandy, my ride or die, had finally found the rest of their safe houses. Tonight, I would burn the crown jewels in his little network of safe houses. Tonight, I would set fire to the demons of my past.

<hr>

The outside of the warehouse hadn't changed, but I had. Misery still clung to this place like an oily cloud, but I was no longer afraid. I wasn't the same girl they'd yanked out of a van wearing nothing but chains.

My belt held an assortment of knives courtesy of Dagger, additional rounds, and the grenade Gunner handed me before we left. Pull the pin and throw, check. That was literally what he said.

Over my black T-shirt a gun holster crisscrossed my back, complete with two new guns, one from my father and one from Switch. My old gun was tucked away in an ankle holster Ryder handed me earlier.

Strapped to my other ankle was another knife, 'cause as Dagger told me, you can never have too many. Most women would argue that it would be shoes or purses, but the shiny knife brought me a sense of security that no purse or shoe ever had.

"You okay?" Switch asked from beside me.

I'd jokingly said Delilah thought she was *Lara Croft*, but I looked the part. It made me feel like I could fuck the world up and walk away. Which was exactly what I intended to do.

"Never better."

A rifle shot broke the stillness of the night and one of the guards by the front door dropped. The rest of the men scurried around like rats. Yes boys, you should be running.

We slipped through the same spot in the fence and started shooting anyone who came at us. Switch was annoyingly accurate, but I didn't sweat it. Whether it was his bullet or mine no longer mattered to me because the result was the same.

Inside the front door, more men came running, and they all met the same fate. Each fallen guard put me closer to my goal, setting the women free.

In the main holding area, I grabbed a set of keys from the pocket of a dead guard and started opening cell doors. With each woman who tentatively stepped forward, afraid to hope that their suffering was at an end, I felt lighter, freer.

Tweak came behind me, handing out T-shirts to all the women. When the last one stepped out of her cage, I looked up at the ceiling, spread my arms wide, and laughed. Maybe Delilah was right, and I was more crazy than smart. That was fine by me. This was the most normal I'd felt since I was first taken.

On our way out, Gunner let me press the button to ignite the C-4 he'd wired the building with. From outside the gates, I watched my nightmare blow up. Burn baby burn. We couldn't stick around for long because someone had to have heard that explosion. With one last look over my shoulder, I let go of all the horror and pain.

Fire was a type of rebirth, or so I'd heard, but I believed it to be true. At least for me. Tonight marked a new chapter of my life. One where the old Stella and the woman I'd become could live in harmony. Neither overshadowing the other. Melded together and stronger for it.

We hit a total of six warehouses just like the one they'd kept me in, and as I'd ridden away, watching each one burn from my rearview mirror, I felt a renewed sense of purpose. Vanload after vanload of women were now free to go back to their old lives or forge new ones.

Whenever I opened a cell door, and the woman inside would cower, I'd think about the promise I'd made to Bree, the first girl Switch and I saved. That I would kill them all. That I would keep her safe.

Only now, there were a lot more than just her that needed to be kept safe. Which was why instead of being sound asleep in bed next to Switch, I was sitting on Brandy's porch swing. The same one Switch had slept on. Though, how he slept on this thing at all was a mystery to me.

The breeze teased the ends of my hair as I sat out here, keeping the night air from becoming muggy. Stars speckled the night sky, the moon full and glowing brightly above me. The crickets kept me company, their song filling the night air.

It should have brought me peace. Instead, the same thought kept turning around inside my brain, clinging like a vine, choking me with uncertainty. What if something happened to one of the women we saved tonight, or one of the women in my family, because I was hell-bent on having my cake and eating it too? What was I willing to risk in the name of vengeance?

A twig snapped to my left, and I sucked in a breath, my chest seizing. The outline of a man formed from the shadows, his profile too bloated and squat to be Hunter or Switch.

"You are a hard woman to track down, Miss McKenzie. It was a stroke of luck that Mateo happened to call me with your location before The Deviants killed him."

His voice carried up the steps, his tone condescending and familiar. Antonio's business partner, Stephen Day. The man whose destruction I'd been contemplating. In a bit of irony, he'd caught me alone, unaware, and without a weapon.

That was life for you, though. A cold hard bitch that slapped you when you least expected it. I'd already tempted fate once with Antonio and survived. I doubted I'd get that lucky again.

"You're nothing but a filthy, repulsive little cockroach that's scurried to my doorstep."

"Everyone knows a cockroach can survive the apocalypse, while you Miss McKenzie, won't survive the next five minutes, so I'll take that as a compliment," he snapped. "And without your father's club here to protect you, you're nothing but a girl who doesn't know when to shut your mouth."

"Pretty strong words coming from a man who plans to shoot an unarmed woman because he's afraid of getting his ass kicked."

It was a bold move, but right now it was the only way I could see myself making it out of this alive. Not that I expected him to take the bait. He made his living by selling something that wasn't his to sell. Why would he suddenly decide to fight fair?

"Clever girl, but I can't be so easily manipulated. I'm not one of your Neanderthals who only know how to solve problems with their fists."

"Oh, I wouldn't say that." My heart kicked into overdrive at the sound of Switch's voice in the darkness. "I'm pretty handy with a gun, too."

He'd come for me. Just like he said he would. Part of me was relieved because frankly, I wasn't ready to die, but mostly I was afraid. Switch was a hell of a shot, but nobody could outrun a bullet. It seemed cruel that after all these years, I finally had him, only to lose him.

"Ah, you have a champion, I see. And a foolish one at that." He whistled, and another figure took shape out in the darkness, the sound of a gun cocking loud in the still night air. "Check mate, Miss McKenzie."

No.

Another gun cocked. "If I were you, Mr. Fancy Pants, I'd call off your dog. No need for him to die along with you."

I'd never been happier to hear my father's voice in all my life. Until Stephen Day laughed.

Then an icy shiver of dread slid down my spine.

"You're even more stupid than I thought if you believe he's the only man I brought with me."

"Now, I think I've had just about enough of you insulting my family," Pops's southern drawl came from the opposite direction.

"I might only be a Neanderthal, but I'd say what we have here is a good old-fashioned standoff," my father said. "What do you think, Hunter?"

"To have a standoff I believe they'd need to have more men."

Hunter's bored voice sounded like it came from beside that asshole, Day. His indrawn breath a second later confirmed my suspicions.

"Who's the dummy now," my father taunted, his tone smug.

"Stel?" Switch was asking what I wanted them to do. I preferred to show them.

The porch swing rocked backward as I stood, my bare feet soundless on the wood as I came down Hunter's steps. When I was close enough to smell the asshole's breath, I held out my hand, and someone placed a blade in the center of my palm. I tested its weight before pushing it against Stephen Day's fleshy neck.

"I hope you enjoy your stay in hell, Mr. Day."

CHAPTER 33

SWITCH

I looked up at the clubhouse as I ground the butt of my cigarette underneath my boot. Ryder was expecting me to attend church this afternoon, though I couldn't imagine why. We'd burned the last of the safe houses, killed all the men involved with the human trafficking ring, and reunited the women with their families.

Hunter and I disposed of the last of the bodies the night before, though he was less than enthusiastic about waxing nostalgic while we dug holes. Not that Hunter ever got excited about much of anything.

Nomads didn't have the right to vote, but we were still members, so nobody, not even a club president, could ask us to leave. Which Ryder already knew, so he couldn't be calling me up here on club business or to kick me out. I suppose he could ask me to stay away from Stel, but I think we both knew what my answer to that was going to be. What in the hell else was there?

Cherry smiled and waved when she saw me, while Valentina did a half turn on her barstool, nodded, then turned right back around. Ryder had always liked his women bitchy, so I got the attraction there, but how the ice princess and cheerleader barbie wound up being friends was beyond me. Girls like Valentina ate girls like Cherry for breakfast, they didn't befriend them.

Oh, to be a fly on the wall tomorrow when Delilah got thrown in with these two. It would be something akin to a wolf, a bunny, and a mole all hanging out together in the woods. Voluntarily, I might add since the wolf and the bunny did say they'd keep an eye on our fragile little mole while Brandy and Stel were down in the shop. None of us trusted Delilah to be by herself, and she didn't leave for the facility she picked out in Arizona until next week.

Shaking my head at myself for my woodland creature's comparison, I headed for the murmur of male voices. Damn, I must be more tired than I thought after last night.

Like the first time I walked into church hell-bent on rescuing my girl, everyone turned and stared. You'd think the novelty of me being at the table would have worn off by now.

Then again, maybe they'd been expecting to see Stel? Ryder hadn't asked for her, so I assumed he wanted to talk to me. But it was possible I'd misunderstood him.

"You want me to go downstairs and get Stel?"

Ryder shook his head. "Nah. She's got a lot of catching up to do down in the shop."

"We're just not used to seeing only one half of Stwitch, anymore," Tweak said with a grin as he looked down at the phone in his lap.

I was probably going to regret asking this question, but what the hell.

"Stwitch?"

He looked up. "Come on, man. Keep up. Stella and Switch. Stwitch."

"Did you start huffing paint down in the shop after I left?"

"We wish it was paint." Gunner rolled his eyes. "Some girl he was fucking showed him this name combiner app and now Trisha and me are Trinner, Hunter and Brandy are Handy, and Valentina and Ryder are Vader. We're worried this girl might actually be a teenager."

"Fuck off, she was twenty-one," Tweak huffed. "Beast will vouch for me."

Beast chuckled. "She did have a drink in her hand when he met her, but I'd like to state for the record that I did not personally check this girl's ID."

Hunter sighed and added, "I don't care how he got this annoying new habit. Only that he won't stop using these ridiculous names, even when I threatened to cut off his finger."

Knowing Hunter, he was dead serious about the finger thing.

"If some girl ever clips my balls, you fuckers better give us a cool nickname."

Ryder pointed at his cousin. "I hope her name is some shit like Boomquifa so we can call you Tweamquif."

Everyone started cracking up, and by the time Ryder banged his gavel I was wiping moisture from underneath my eye with my thumb. Damn, I'd missed these assholes.

"We've had our fun, and now it's time to get down to business. Switch, I asked you here because the fellas wanted to vote on a matter that concerns you."

What the fuck could he be talking about? The only thing that concerned me was Stel. Was she still in danger? Had we missed something?

"All in favor of Switch being reinstated as a member of the San Antonio charter, raise your hands."

As I looked around the table, one man after another started to raise their hand. By the time I'd gotten all the way around to Ryder, he had his hand in the air too. Damn. Every single one of them had voted for me to be a member. They were going to give me another chance, just like Stel. I couldn't believe it.

Ryder banged the gavel again and stood, his eyes meeting mine. "I didn't think I could ever forgive you for putting the club in danger, but I put my feelings aside for Stella. We all did. It wasn't until you saved my life that I finally realized what Pops had been trying to tell me. You've always had love for me and this club, but Stella was the one thing you couldn't stand to live without. Now that I have a wife of my own, I get it."

His lips tipped up in the corner. "So, what do you say? We could certainly use a man like you down in the shop."

"I'd love to, man. You have no idea how much having a home with you guys means to me."

And they really didn't. It wasn't until after Stel was safe that I realized a part of my being lost had nothing to do with her. She would always come first in my life, but I needed the purpose and strength these men gave me.

When I belonged to the Tucson charter, I did my part and pushed their drugs, but it wasn't the same. They didn't have the camaraderie and fellowship these men did. They didn't look out for each other or give a fuck when one of 'em was dying more and more each day. I wanted to take care of them the way I wanted to take care of Stel, knowing that they would do the same for me.

"Glad to have you back, buddy." He raised the gavel, preparing to bring it down. Now was my chance to do right by Stel, even if it meant giving up what I'd just gotten back. "If there's nothing else…"

"Yeah, actually there is." Ryder nodded for me to continue, and I stood. "I move that Stella be allowed to prospect. She loves this club every bit as much as any of us and she's proven her worth time and time again. Should she want the chance, I think she deserves it."

All the men were silent, none of them even looking around the table. This didn't bode well for my motion. Then Beast stroked a hand down his dark beard and cleared his throat.

"With all due respect, I don't think Stella should prospect."

This motherfucker. I took a step forward, and he held up his hand.

"Let me finish. You're right. The girl could barely stand and had to be carried out by Hunter, yet she still cut a man's dick off. If that doesn't embody what a Devil is, then I'm in the wrong place. I think it's high time we unleash her on our enemies and let them feel her wrath. I move to consider her prospecting period complete and proceed with her membership."

It was an unprecedented move. Everyone prospected for the club for a year, even Ryder. Female Devil's weren't unheard of, but they weren't exactly commonplace either. I'd only heard of the club having one female officer, and she was a legend, but if anyone could best her, it would be Stel.

Tweak raised his hand. "I have something I'd like to add."

Ryder inclined his head, giving Tweak the floor. Which was a little baffling to me because Tweak never asked permission for anything. He got by with talking out of turn 'cause he was charming and Ryder's cousin. Not that what he had to say wasn't worthwhile. You just sometimes had to wade through a little bullshit to get to it.

"Last night I caught Stella standing there, staring into an empty cell. She told me she had a nail in her hand when she arrived at the warehouse. When she saw Delilah, she knew if they could take a man like Jules's family, then they could get to ours. She imagined Cherry in Delilah's place, watching the light being sucked from her eyes until there was nothing left, and she dropped the nail."

His dark eyes scanned the room. "She was ashamed that she'd been too weak to tell Hunter to leave her there, so she made a promise to herself that she wouldn't rest until the last cell sat empty."

Pride swelled within my chest. My girl had no clue how fucking amazing she truly was.

"Stella suffered trying to protect the women

in our care. She made sure we wouldn't fail. That took more balls than any of us at this table have, so I wholeheartedly second Beast's motion."

When Tweak finished, there wasn't a man sitting at the table with dry eyes. Outlaw bikers were moved by the bravery of my woman. I wished she were here to see it, able to see the pride on her father's face.

"Yes, well…" Ryder coughed. "Show of hands."

Hands flew into the air and Ryder smacked his gavel down sealing Stel's fate. My girl was to be a Devil. Something I knew she'd always been at her heart.

"I need a beer," Mad Dog muttered and clapped me on the shoulder on his way out.

He wasn't the only one who needed something to take the edge off his emotions. It had been hours since I'd laid a hand on my girl. Besides, she could use a break. She'd been working hard all morning and now she'd have me to help her catch up.

When I went downstairs, I found her bent over the front of a '66 Mustang. The left strap of her overalls had slid over her shoulder, revealing the white tank top she wore beneath. Fuck me, there was no bra strap beneath it, either. My mouth watered. I'd always wanted to fuck her against the hood of a car.

She looked over her shoulder and smiled, wiping a hand across her brow, leaving a trail of sand behind. God, she was beautiful.

My feet moved of their own accord toward the only thing I'd ever coveted. Stella McKenzie. Soon to be Stella Clayton if I had anything to say about it.

She turned around, and I grabbed her by the hips, setting her on the hood.

"What are you doing?"

Her voice had that breathless quality she got whenever she was turned on. I fucking loved that shit.

"Taking what's mine."

It was the god's honest truth. She'd been mine since we were kids and now that we were grown that hadn't changed.

My lips grazed her neck, and she tipped her head back to give me better access, a moan escaping her lips. Against the front of my jeans my cock jumped, itching to be nestled in her heat.

Her hands bunched in my shirt, her nails digging in, as I pushed the straps of her overalls down. When I reached her waist, I searched for the hem of her tank top, yanking it up to bare her rosy nipples to my waiting mouth.

She gasped as I sucked the stiff peak, her sweet taste filling my mouth.

Over the heavy metal that played in the background, I heard Tweak shout, "What the fuck, Stwitch!"

My lips left her nipple long enough to shout,

"Fuck off," before losing myself in her delectable flesh.

"Fine! But when I get back, we're setting up some fucking ground rules for the shop!"

Stel laughed as he walked away, the sound vibrating the nipple I had a hold of. I pulled her closer, tugging on her coveralls. Her laugh faded to a moan as she lifted her ass up to let me slide them off. I released her and took a step back to have a look.

Fuck me. She sat on the hood, her tank top was around her neck, her nipple stiff and wet from my attention, a bit of black lace covering her pussy. She was a goddess. Every man's wet dream come to life.

My finger hooked the lace and tore one side of it.

"Hey!"

"You won't be needing these," I said as I tore the other side, revealing her perfect pink pussy.

My hand slid up her stomach to her chest and pushed her back against the hood. Fuck yeah. Her heels pressed into the hood on either side of me as I leaned forward. She tasted of heaven, sweet and tangy.

She writhed against the hood, her hands absently digging in as I ate her out, her moans turning into screams. Her juices hit my tongue as she came, and I eagerly licked her pussy, trying to soak up every last drop. She was fucking delicious.

She grabbed my hair, her legs shaking as she pulled. I looked up at her molten honey eyes.

"Get up here and fuck me."

Who was I to argue? Especially when it was what I'd been waiting to do, anyway.

"Yes, ma'am," I murmured as I pulled my jeans down enough to free my cock.

She looked down her body, her eyes watching as my cock nudged her entrance. I slammed into her pussy, watching her head fall back and her body shift upward on the hood. Grabbing on to her hips, I slid out and rocked back into her. Sensation drowned me and it was the best feeling in the world.

I got lost in fucking my girl, claiming her as I'd always wanted. It was rough, raw, and utterly mind blowing. She moved with me, undulating against the hood, taking everything I gave her.

Her pussy clamped down around me, her lips parted, as she screamed, "Switch!"

My release came out of nowhere, slamming into me, robbing me of breath. This right here was everything. She was everything.

Her honeyed eyes met mine, and I blurted, "Marry me. I want you to be my old lady in every sense of the word."

She stilled, her eyes widening.

My heart beat out of my chest as I added, "I'll get you a fat diamond. A house. Anything you want. Just say yes."

She sat up, my dick slipping out of her, and a

sinking feeling started in the pit of my stomach. Her hands stroked either side of my beard.

"No diamond."

Shit. Here I was a grown man, an outlaw biker, and I wanted to bawl my eyes out. My girl was trying to let me down easy because she wasn't ready to be mine. At least, not in the binding forever kinda way that I wanted her to be.

"A ring will only get in my way. I'd rather have a tattoo on my ring finger."

Wait. What?

"Is that a yes?" I asked, hope blooming in my chest.

She smirked. "How else am I going to make sure you never leave me again?"

I crushed her to me, peppering kisses along her cheekbones. Joy filled me near to bursting.

"Until death do us part," I vowed in between kisses, smiling against her skin. "And even then, I'd follow you into the fires of hell because that's where all The Devil's Deviants go when we die."

Her breath caught, her hands pulling on my hair, so I'd look her in the eye. "They took you back?"

"Yes, but that's not what I was trying to tell you." Confusion crinkled her brow, and it was fucking adorable. Tweak better not come back anytime soon 'cause Stel and I had a lot of celebrating to do. "Welcome to The Deviants, Wild Thing."

If you enjoyed Switch, and his Wild Thing, Stella, then you will love Pops and Cat. After all of these years alone, Pops finds himself torn between the club he created and the woman he shouldn't want in BURNED.

FREE bonus scene from Switch when you join Gladys After Dark.

ABOUT THE AUTHOR

"Gray is my favorite color and sarcasm is my second language."

Gladys Cross lives in South Carolina with her husband, two children, and furbaby. When she isn't dipping her toe into the darker side of love, you'll find her reading, beating her family at cards, petting goats, or spending time outdoors.

www.gladysafterdark.com

Made in the USA
Las Vegas, NV
25 May 2024

90372366R00164